THE
NOXHELM
MURDERS

DR. BON BLOSSMAN

First Paperback Edition: October 2017

The characters and events portrayed in this novel are fictitious. Any
similarity to real persons, alive or dead, is coincidental and not
intended by the author.

Blossman, Bon 1970—

ISBN: 0-9965248-5-1
ISBN-13: 978-0-9965248-5-8

DEDICATION

I dedicate this book to Rhythm Myer Overbey.

CONTENTS

ACKNOWLEDGMENTS

I wish to thank my soul mate and husband, Jason, for the years of never-ending support and love.

Thank you to my wonderful niece, Ella, for agreeing to be the spooky ghost on the cover – you rocked it, as always.

To my other lovely nieces, Madison, Lauren, and Aubrey – you are awesome. I hope you love this book!

Rhythm Myer Overbey – you are the best g-baby I could have ever asked for, and I love you to the moon and back. Whitney and Zakk – you are my world, and you continue to inspire me on a daily basis. I love you so much!

There isn't enough space on this page to thank everyone I want to thank, but I will make a short list here of those who are standing out in my brain at the moment: Brandon, Susan, Dana, Sylvia, Bronnie-Jo, Gemma – you guys are always the first to read my books, and I can't put into words how much I appreciate you.

Alex, thank you for agreeing to play the role of Shana Murphy in the book trailer. You are beyond awesome.

Thanks to Eric and Katy for all your input on the cover!

Mom and Dad – thank you once again for your love and support. I hope this book doesn't give you nightmares, Mom!

1-MR. FLYNN

I dropped to my knees next to my pit bull; blood seeped from a gaping wound in his abdomen as he labored for his next breath.

"Who did this to you, Hugo?" Tears gushed from my eyes as I heaved for air. I stormed into the living room, and a sudden coldness hit my core as I witnessed Maurice Flynn wrap a chain around my father's neck. With black spots forming in my vision, I fought to remain conscious, bracing myself against the back of the sofa.

"Maurice, we don't gotta do this," my dad said as he struggled for his next breath, his fingers turning white underneath the ligature.

"I have orders, Cullen. You know the deal."

My father broke free, spun around, and shoved his attacker with both hands. My legs trembled. I had no clue how to help.

"Mr. Flynn, why are you doing this? Leave him alone!" I screamed until my throat burned like fire.

My parents' bedroom door crashed against the

wall, and my mother's footsteps sounded down the hallway. Still lying on the ground in the foyer next to a wide-open door, Hugo wheezed with a gurgled breath and then was silent. A wave of nausea incapacitated me.

"Sorry, Shana, but Pops here shoulda kept his mouth shut on business matters. I hate to do this to ya, sweetheart."

Since I could remember, I had always loved Mr. Flynn and considered him a part of our family. "Please don't."

My father struck his jaw with a left hook, and he stumbled backward, his fedora sailing into the air as the garrote clanked against the white marble floor tile. Mr. Flynn pulled a switchblade from his back pocket as he balanced himself. He pushed the trigger to release the blade. I ground my teeth as my eyes caught Hugo's bloodstains on the knife's edge.

Mr. Flynn dove for my father, and they tumbled to the ground. My dad's head collided with the hard floor, and his eyes rolled into the backs of their sockets for a split second. My mother approached with terror plaguing her face. A stronger wave of nausea struck, causing me to gag. With my hand to my throat, I steadied myself.

"Mom, he hurt Hugo, and now he's after Dad!" Hysterical, I took short breaths to calm my spinning brain.

"Maurice!" My mother sprinted toward the men on the ground.

Straddling my father, Mr. Flynn fought for

control of the weapon as my mother clutched tufts of his hair. He was unfazed. A malevolent grin spread across his face as he used all his strength to move the knife toward my father's chest.

"Stop it! You'll kill him!"

My head jerked toward a $38,000 Baccarat antique I had been warned many times never to touch. I had always been drawn to the piece, as if I knew that one day I'd use it for something important. I ignored the price tag as my fingers wrapped around the stem of the vase, and the dense crystal turned weightless in my hand. My surroundings faded away to black, and the sound muted. The next thing I can remember is my mother's piercing scream as Mr. Flynn tumbled onto the sheepskin rug with blood oozing from the back of his head. My father scrambled to his feet. I stared at what I had accomplished, unable to look away. My heartbeat pounded my eardrums as I waited for Mr. Flynn's last breath, but it never came.

"Shana, go," my mother said as she snatched the switchblade from the unconscious man.

A sharp pain exploded inside my wrist, and the sweat from my palm made it easy for the vase to slide from my hand and onto the floor.

She checked Mr. Flynn's vitals. "He's alive, Cullen."

My father ripped down drapery cords from the windows.

"What about Hugo? Should we call the vet?" I asked. I was in denial that he was gone.

"That won't be necessary. Go to your room," my mother said, turning Mr. Flynn's body over. His head was soaked in blood. "We'll handle this mess."

"I should've known Vince would turn on me."

"Cullen, you've been nothing but loyal. Maybe Maurice did this on his own?"

My dad used the cords to tie Mr. Flynn's hands together behind his back. I was immobilized as I weighed the gravity of my actions. I had nearly killed a man. Everything was surreal, as if I had just hopped inside a television show.

"Shana, now," my mother said in a grave tone.

I moved toward the foyer with slow steps. As I passed my dog, my eyes produced a new batch of tears. Hugo's body had already started to stiffen as he stared unwaveringly into the black sky through the front door. At least he wasn't suffering.

Sirens rang in the distance. "The neighbors must have called the police," my mother said, her face reddening.

"No turning back now. Plan B," my dad said.

"Are you sure? There's no other way?"

My parents spewed obscenities as they paced back and forth around the body. From the blackness of night, a red light flickered, followed by blue. The sirens blared louder.

"Mom, Dad. The police are here. What do you want me to do?"

Tires screeched as the spinning strobes halted in the street. The moonlight hit my neighbor's white pajamas — she stood like a wraith in our front yard, trying to peep inside. "Should I close the door?" I eyeballed whether I could clear Hugo's body with the door as I grabbed the doorknob.

"No, Shana, it's too late for that. Go to your room. I won't say it again," my mother said.

My world started to spin, and tears dripped from my chin. My feet trailed Hugo's blood down the hallway and into my bedroom. After a shuffling of footsteps, I heard muffled voices, but I couldn't decipher the words. With uncontrolled sobs, I tried to make sense of what had happened. In my days, I had seen more than the average seventeen-year-old, but this was serious. This was different. This kind of thing didn't happen to an O'Sullivan—not in Boston, anyway.

After a few minutes, someone knocked on my door. A chill shivered down my spine. I hesitated, as I could tell it wasn't either of my parents.

"Um, yes? Come in." I scrunched myself up as small as I could on my lounger.

A uniformed cop entered the room. "Shana O'Sullivan?"

She couldn't have been more than twenty-five, with meticulous makeup and a long ponytail jutting out beneath a traditional police cap.

"Yes, ma'am. I'm Shana."

I gave her a quick, false smile and listened intently.

"My name is Officer Ali Horn with the Boston PD."

"Okay, thanks."

My scalp prickled as I realized how dumb my words were. I had no experience speaking with the police, and my father had never spoken too highly of them.

"May I take a seat?" Officer Ali gestured to the chair next to mine.

"Yes, I guess so." After a quick glance, I moved my eyes to the ceiling as I combed my fingers through my hair, then dried off my cheeks with my sleeves. The officer took a moment to observe my behavior, and it seemed like an eternity. I chewed on my fingernail, crossed and uncrossed my arms and legs, and tugged my clothes into place until she spoke again.

"Shana, I need you to tell me what happened, in your own words."

I deliberated about what to say as I stared out my patio door at the full moon. Dropping my head to the floor, I cringed at the blood coating my feet. A quick scan of my body revealed splatter from Mr. Flynn's head on my right arm. I flinched with a hard swallow. Then it hit me.

"Are my parents all right with me talking to you? May I speak to my mother first?" The words came out with a high pitch, as if someone had pushed "Fast-forward."

"Shana, you're not in trouble, honey. I just need a statement from you on what happened tonight. You are a minor, so feel free to speak to your parents if you need to do so."

Officer Ali was calm, her words even, her

emotions steadfast. I trusted her, so I decided to talk.

"I woke up—"

My father burst through the door. "My daughter will not speak to cops without an attorney present. Shana, not another word."

He could be menacing, and he had a hot temper. My dad knew the law well—he'd had his share of tangles with the police.

"But she just wants to hear my side—"

His eyes burned into mine, and I hushed as my stomach churned hot lava. I turned back toward the patio door and stared into the night sky.

"I'm afraid we will need to ask your family to come down to the station, Mr. O'Sullivan. Without official statements from all parties, we can't close this investigation. The victim was in pretty bad shape and may die. If so, this case may change to a homicide."

My father took a calming breath and exhaled slowly. He pulled his mobile phone from his pocket, called his attorney, and put the call on speaker.

"Hello," the tired voice on the other end of the phone said.

"Richard, can you meet me at the police station in fifteen?

"Cullen, for you, I'll be there in ten," he said.

2-WITSEC

"I'm tired. Can't we just stay home? Mr. Flynn's at the hospital — we're safe now."

A limousine pulled up in front of our home. I sighed as I climbed inside. I searched for an excuse not to go with my parents to the police station, but I couldn't settle on one they would buy.

"Shana, it isn't up for debate. We have to play this right," my father said. I always thought his hair flamed a brighter ginger when he was annoyed.

"Why do we have to go? It's past midnight, they already took forever snooping around our house, and I have a test in art history tomorrow. We're the victims. Don't they understand that?"

My father pressed his freckled hands into a ball and shook his head. "Yes, they do. That's why we're not in cuffs, Shana. We're going there voluntarily, in our own transportation. Our family doesn't speak to police without Mr. Nugent. Skip school tomorrow to catch up on sleep."

"Deal." I fumbled through the selection of sodas

in the tray and fished out a Dr Pepper from underneath the ice.

"Cullen, over there," my mother said as she pointed out the window.

My father's boss owned a fleet of Cadillac Escalades, all with dark-tinted windows. When I spun around to see what my mother was pointing at, one of them was driving by our house. My parents seemed nervous about it, but it was normal to me. There were always black SUVs around us.

"Driver, let's go, now."

My mother's face turned grim. Something inside her was broken. Even with flawlessly applied cosmetics and flapper-inspired hair, something prevented her from being composed for the first time. She had always preached that a smile was the final accessory, but she wasn't wearing one.

My dad leaned in toward her. "Courtney, it's got to be the stupid neighbors. Now we gotta do it this way." He whispered, but my young ears caught every word.

I pretended to browse on my cell phone even though the battery was dead.

"Cullen, why'd Maurice turn? Did Vince put a hit out on you?" my mom asked with a quivering lip. "Why would he do that?"

He hesitated, gazing over to see if I was eavesdropping.

"I spoke out against Lapse. Didn't think we should be selling synthetic opiates to kids. I refused to be a part of the game and tried to talk the guys out of supporting it." He dropped his head. "My grandfather's turning over in his grave right now with the direction that Vince's taken everything." He sat upright again and pressed his face against the glass to see if the SUV was tailing us.

I was unfamiliar with the term Lapse, as I didn't run with the kids who did those sorts of things. I had learned about most drugs from a sixth-grade seminar with Barry the Crime Bear, and my best friend, Monica, and I had vowed to stay clear of them.

"That doesn't seem like a motive to put a hit on you, Cullen. Maybe this has something to do with Candy?"

I despised my aunt Candy. She had left my uncle Cillian for another man—my dad and uncle's boss. She was the sole reason why Cillian had been murdered, and I never wanted to see her again.

"Nah, I've played cool on that front, Courtney, but it's taken every fiber in my body to stop me from strangling Vince since it all went down. At the funeral, I did everything I could not to shoot him between the eyes, right there in front of everyone. But there's no way this is about the Candy situation. I'm telling you—Maurice squealed that I was against getting involved with Lapse. I've felt like something's been off with him lately, and now I see my hunch was right."

"The sting of betrayal is harsh, Cullen. What'll we do now? Move?"

My father shot her a cautioning look and nodded

his head toward me. They did their best to shield me from things, but I was perceptive — to my detriment. The thought of moving away from my friends only weeks away from my high school graduation was a nightmare. He checked for the SUV again. Judging by the look on his face, we had a tail. The hum of the engine took center stage for the next few minutes until we pulled into the parking lot of the police station.

"Drop us right by the front door, and no need to wait," my father said.

"This should be fun," my mother said as she reapplied her red lipstick.

I flipped down the mirror in the back of the limo's ceiling to check my face. I expected the pasty eggshell skin with red, swollen eyes but was surprised that my hair was still silky straight from the day before. I refused to be in public when it curled, as I couldn't stand being called Clown Wig — a nickname that had emerged after I chopped it to my shoulders. On humid days, it would turn bushy and stick straight out from my head. My dad expedited our move from the limo to the front door. Just as he opened the lobby door, the Escalade drove by the parking lot slowly.

"Shana, tell the truth, but keep it short and sweet. Follow Mr. Nugent's instructions. If he says not to answer, don't say a word. You hear me?"

"Yes, Dad. I got it. I've seen interrogations on TV shows."

He chuckled as we approached his attorney, who

had been waiting in the foyer. Richard Nugent was thick through the middle, midfifties, and he wore a sharp gray suit. His eyes were blue on a canvas of red lines that suggested a history of sleepless nights.

"Ah, Richard. Thank you for coming on short notice," my dad said with a stern handshake.

"Mr. O'Sullivan, it's my pleasure. I spoke to a lady officer, and she told me a prowler killed the family dog and attacked you?"

"That sums it up, but the intruder was Maurice Flynn."

Mr. Nugent's eyes filled with dread as he stared at my father. He clenched his jaw so tight, his pulse thumped in his temples. The silence went on for at least a minute. They seemed to communicate telepathically.

Officer Ali stuck her head out from behind a door. "Mr. and Mrs. O'Sullivan, please come with me. Shana, you, too." She nodded at Mr. Nugent. "Follow me."

We trailed the officer down a white-walled corridor and entered a room with a black table and four mismatched chairs. There was a window that revealed a small room with a height chart painted on the wall. I supposed this was used for identifying suspects from a lineup.

"Hold on a minute, folks. Let me grab more chairs," Officer Ali said before she rushed out the door.

"This place is a dump," I said.

"It's not a place where they want you to feel

welcome, Shana," my mother said.

She returned with two tattered stools, and we grouped around the table. The moment Officer Ali tried to speak, our attorney cut her off.

"My client is willing to testify against Vincent Byrne for multiple counts of extortion, racketeering, and murder in exchange for blanket immunity and placement into the United States Federal Witness Protection Program. I understand you are local law enforcement and cannot make this deal, but we will wait here while you contact the appropriate agency."

Officer Ali's face flushed, and her mouth gaped. She turned her head to the side as she studied Mr. Nugent. A rookie beat officer; she was taken aback by his requests. "I have brought your clients here to discuss an incident that happened at their home earlier this evening." After an awkward pause, she continued. "I don't know what this has to do with Vincent Byrne, but I need to interview your clients about the sequence of events that occurred between Cullen Sullivan and Maurice Flynn." Mr. Nugent stared at her without blinking or saying a word. "The victim is in surgery right now and may not make it. It is critical that we know exactly what happened tonight on Beacon Street."

My parents sat still as statues, and neither showed a glimmer of emotion. Mr. Nugent sat up in his chair and rubbed the back of his neck.

"WITSEC was formally established under Title V of the Organized Crime Control Act of 1970. The attorney general has an open RICO case on Vincent Byrne but hasn't found enough evidence to convict. I'm sure you are familiar with RICO, right?" Officer Ali stared at Mr. Nugent with a blank expression. "It's The Racketeer Influenced and Corrupt Organizations Act, which is a federal law, put in place for extended criminal penalties for being involved with underground operations. My client's testimony ensures a conviction. The program defines how the AG may provide for the relocation and protection of a witness of the federal government in an official proceeding concerning organized crime. You can refer to 18 US Code 3521 for further details, or I can go over them with you now. Either way, my clients will be taking advantage of their civil liberties, Officer Ali Horn. Call your DOJ contact. I am giving you notice it is not safe for my clients to even be in this police station. The quicker you can expedite this situation, the safer every officer in this building will be."

3-THE JOURNEY

I took a nap on the couch in the break room while the adults covered the fine details. My parents woke me at 2:35 a.m., and we were escorted by a team of uniformed officers into a Lincoln Navigator in the back parking lot. They had negotiated Mr. Nugent's proposal, but I was unsure what that would mean for me.

"Mom, what's going on? We're not moving away from Boston, are we?"

She inhaled a deep breath through her nose. "Shana, be mature about this. Let's not fight."

Climbing into the back seat, I was under silent protest. I just wanted to go home. My phone was dead, and I couldn't contact my friends.

"Let me see your phone, Mom."

"No. We'll get all the details at the DOJ office, but we've been given firm instructions not to contact anyone for now."

"What? Are you joking?"

"Shana, that's enough. Not another word," my

father boomed.

I wanted to throw a fit worthy of a toddler, but he didn't put up with nonsense. I couldn't imagine moving away without at least speaking to my friends about what had just happened to me. I had lived in Boston my entire life. I loved my luxurious brownstone two doors down from my best friend, my personal shoppers at my favorite department stores, and my favorite seafood restaurant. I had finally lucked into an easy school schedule with the best teachers, and I was so close to graduating with my best childhood friends. My brain couldn't process leaving without saying goodbye. I thought I would explode from the inside.

The SUV pulled up into the parking garage of a large, dark building. Suited agents ushered us into a conference room with plush furniture. It reminded me of the boardroom on The Apprentice television show. The clock on the wall read 3:14 a.m. As they sorted through manila folders and files, I folded my arms on the table and rested my head. Their voices faded off into the distance as my heavy eyelids closed.

"Shana, wake up," my mother said as she nudged my shoulder.

It took a few seconds for me to realize where I was, and that I wasn't waking from a nightmare.

"Can we go home?" I rubbed a crick in my neck. A woman wearing a black shirt with a white star on it sat beside me.

"Shana, my name is Jenna Bronaugh. I'm with the US Marshals Service. I work with the attorney general to place families in safe homes during times of trouble."

"I don't want to leave Boston. I graduate in a few weeks. I can't abandon my friends."

My dad pounded a fist on the table. "Shana, listen to Deputy Bronaugh. You have no other option."

"Okay." I bit my quivering lip.

"We have taken your mobile devices and all pieces of identification, and will return all of your possessions after the trial."

"Um, I need my license. No matter where we go, I'll have to drive."

She handed me a bulging manila folder. "Here is your packet. It contains a new birth certificate, driver's license, social security card, and school records."

"What about a phone? My laptop?"

"Your parents will purchase new devices. We can't risk any of your software having GPS or any other type of location applications. Do not log on to any of your e-mail or social media accounts or contact acquaintances while you are in the program. Do not post any pictures of yourself or your former name online. If you do, your family's safety will be in jeopardy. It is an inconvenience, but just until the trial is over and you're safe."

"My dad owns a gun range. He has to work. We can't leave."

"We are taking care of your family's finances

until your parents can establish a sufficient income in the new location."

"I have no clothes, makeup, or hair stuff. I need to go home and pack."

"Shana, you cannot go back home. It's not safe. We've taken care of everything to get you through a few days. You each have a packed suitcase with clothing and hygiene products. You can go shopping once you're settled."

Reality hit me. My throat constricted. Thoughts of storming out of the room flashed through my head, but I had nowhere to go. I sat with slumped shoulders, clenching my jaw to prevent an outburst. My eyes welled up as images of my dog fighting for his life and my dad with a chain around his neck surfaced in my mind. All I wanted to do was cry. This situation was abysmal.

"Are you going to tell my friends? They'll ask questions. They won't just let it go. Monica will not accept that I disappeared."

"You can tell them everything once you return."

I moaned. "How long will that be?"

"There is no way for me to answer. It depends solely upon the trial, which hasn't been scheduled."

"Couldn't they just look up the name O'Sullivan online? Once I go to school or Dad opens another gun range, it's all out there. My dad's boss has hackers, you know."

She nodded, and then gazed at my mom and dad. "Your parents can go over your new identity with you, Shana. We've been working with them on techniques on how to forge new friendships and how not to reveal your true identity or raise suspicions. You will need to take some time to learn your new backstory. You can't arrive at the location and do anything questionable, as you'll put your entire family in jeopardy."

We sat in silence for a long moment. A glimmer of hope sparked in my mind.

"Can we at least move to Orlando, Florida? I love Disney and Universal Studios. We vacation there twice a year, and I've always said I'd live there if it weren't Boston."

"That is exactly why you cannot live there, Shana. You'll be traveling to a rather isolated town in the California mountains. It's charming."

"I don't want to live anywhere charming. I want a big city with stuff to do. Are you joking?"

My father cleared his throat and bumped his fist against the table again. "Shana, that's enough. This is hard on all of us, and there's no room for teenage tantrums. We're ready. Let's go," he said with a flushed face and flared nostrils.

"Awesome. Let's go to this charming town."

4-MR. DOYLE

We arrived at Logan International Airport by 11:00 a.m. on Wednesday, May 3. Even though it had been fewer than twelve hours since this nightmare began, it seemed like days had passed — probably because I'd only had a couple of catnaps. A couple of marshals pretended to travel to the same destination to escort us to the plane. They were inconspicuous to avoid drawing attention. My father excused himself to the restroom before we went through the TSA checkpoint. Anxiety grew among us every second he was gone. Mom paced the floor, and the feds were running out of things to do to act ordinary — they had lingered around the flight check-in kiosk, asked the agents at the desk a few questions, bought sodas at the machine, and browsed on their phones. Just as the male agent headed toward the restroom to check on my dad, he bounded out of the restroom.

"Seriously, Cullen." My mother's elbows were held wide from her body with hands on her hips and her chest thrust out.

"You mean Ian, don't you, Bronnie-Jo?" My dad's tone was sarcastic.

She shook her head and gave a false smile. "Ugh. This is going to be more difficult than I imagined. We maybe should have kept our first names like Shana."

"Too late for that, Bronnie-Jo."

The marshals moved ahead of us to a security line, rolling luggage behind them. They flashed a small leather binder to the agent and were allowed to pass through without having to do anything further.

"Ian, what took you so long?" my mother said as we entered the priority boarding queue.

"I spotted Mickey Doyle over there. He was waiting for me. We had discussed plan B right after Vince took over. He's been here since he got the news about Maurice."

"You told Mickey where we are going?"

I gasped. "That's not fair, Mom! Dad told Mr. Doyle, but I can't tell my best friend?"

She glared at me as she wheeled her government-provided suitcase toward the TSA podium. At the time, I believed there would be nothing inside I'd dare to wear. A huge shopping trip was in my future, but I wasn't sad about that.

"Ian, I know you trust Mickey with your life, with all our lives, but you don't know who followed him here—or what they'll do to him if they find out he spoke with you."

"No way he'd allow anyone to follow him. He's smart. Most of the guys take my side and are still loyal to the O'Sullivan name. It's just a few bad seeds. Once we get rid of Vince, I'm taking over like I should have done when Grandfather passed, but I can't do it without Mickey."

Mr. Doyle had been like an uncle to me. I trusted that my father knew what he was doing. He would never intentionally put us in danger.

"Get your boarding passes and IDs ready," my mother said.

We had reached the checkpoint, and the agent held out his hand. I pulled my new driver's license from the manila envelope. My new name was Shana Murphy. My eyes burned from the tears welling in my eyes. I loved being an O'Sullivan. The name had a history, and people respected it where I was from.

After we passed through the body scanners, my dad leaned over toward me. "Shana, I got something for you from Mr. Walsh. A going-away present." He slipped me a big bag of candy. "And this is from Mr. Doyle." He put a brand-new iPhone in my hand. A huge smile spread across my face, lifting my spirits—at least for the moment. I opened the camera on the phone and snapped a selfie. A self-proclaimed historian, I had a thing for taking photos of everything.

"Wait a minute. John Patrick Walsh was with Mickey?" My mother grabbed her luggage from the conveyor belt.

My dad groaned. "Look, these guys are like

family. They are not enemies. If anything, we need to assure them we're on their side, and that I didn't make a deal to squeal on them — it was a good thing we spoke. Trust me. And I didn't tell them where we were headed, so leave it alone." We entered the concourse and looked for the undercover agents we were supposed to follow.

"What about the cell phone you just handed Shana? That can be tracked."

"Again, I trust Mickey with all our lives. It's a nonissue. The feds are right there. Follow them to Gate 24."

My ticket said I was in seat 2C, and I was glad to board the plane in first class, as I was starving and needed rest. The feds had acquired the higher-priced tickets, which was all part of the deal. Mr. Nugent was fierce and a legend for getting blood out of turnips. During the next couple of hours on the connecting flight to Chicago, I caught up on sleep.

5-TURBULENCE

The second leg to Noxhelm was more eventful. I broke out my bag of candy, and it was the most delicious taffy I'd ever tasted. I decided to make it last until I could return home to Boston and buy more, so I came up with a plan to eat a piece only when I missed home and felt sad. It was my sole connection to my former life besides the clothes on my back and my parents.

"D'you mind if I sit here?" a handsome guy with caramel-colored hair and eyes asked as he pointed to the open seat beside me. He was thin, but muscular, and in his later teen years.

"Uh, sure." My parents were asleep across the way. "Sneaking up from coach?" I asked with a laugh.

He slipped down into the aisle seat with a two-dimple smile.

"No, I'm four rows back with my fam, but my stepbrother's getting on my nerves. I need some fresh air before I pop him in the face."

"Ah, I see. Sibling rivalry."

"Oh, there's no rivalry. Take a look at him — he's next to the empty seat."

I stood up, scanned the cabin, and my eyes landed on a frizzy cloud of blond hair. An utter nerd, he wore black-rimmed glasses with a miserable complexion on his pale face. The guy popped his head up and caught me gawking at him, so I dropped back into my seat.

"I'm sure he's smart. He looks like he does very well in math," I said with a smile. "Going to Cali for vacation?"

"No, coming home from a boring week in Chicago. My dad had a business meeting on Saturday, made us tag along for family bonding. I didn't mind missing three days of school, though."

"Did the bonding trip work?"

"What do you think?" He grinned. "What's your name?"

"Shana."

"Just Shana?"

He had an intense stare that made me feel vulnerable, as if he were reading my secrets through my eyes. I clasped my hands together and bounced my knee.

"Shana Murphy," I said, trying not to hesitate. I gave a casual glance out the window, wishing time would speed up.

"Where are you from?"

I shifted in my seat, unable to get comfortable. "Chicago. And you?" Straining to remember my backstory, I dredged up the diversion techniques my parents had taught me during the car ride, but my mind was blank.

"Ah, big-city girl." He tapped my knee with a grin. "Where I'm from, well, it's so lame. A small town with tons of fog. Until I traveled, I thought that's how the world was, but then I realized we're the weird ones."

"What's the town's name?"

"Noxhelm."

Without warning, the plane hit a pocket of turbulence and bounced around in the sky as if we had struck something. My heart raced so fast, I became dizzy. Shrieks and moans sounded from within the cabin, followed by an array of complaints of spilled drinks. With clammy hands, I grabbed the armrests.

"Whoa, that was crazy." A sour taste formed in my mouth. I tried to swallow it away to no avail.

The pilot's voice sounded from the overhead speaker. "We're turning on the seat-belt sign. We expect a bit of turbulence ahead. Flight attendants, please take your seats."

"Wait, what? The flight attendants have to strap in? How bad is it going to get?" I leaned up to get eye contact with my mother for reassurance that everything was all right, but my parents were still sleeping. They must have been dreaming they were riding a roller coaster.

"My name's Blaine Walker, by the way," he said as he caressed my hand that was still vice-gripping the armrest. "Nice to meet you, Shana Murphy."

6-NOXHELM

"No way. I'm not riding in that. Where's the limo?"

"Shana, get in," my father said.

After a few gulps of air, I threw myself across the back seat of a taxicab. I'd never been in one, but I had heard horror stories from friends. People hadn't lied or exaggerated—the car smelled of bologna with a layer of grime that coated everything, and the driver wore a nasty frown on his face. My parents filed in, and we took off to our new address, fitting together snugly.

"It will be at least thirty," the driver mumbled.

"Super," I said.

During the ride in the stench mobile, I distracted myself with a game app I had downloaded on my phone called Monster Madness. The game's objective was to design the ultimate monster to murder criminals in the city, like a vigilante. It was twisted but made the time pass.

As we neared the town, a light mist turned to fog,

which brought back bad feelings from our flight. Before long we could barely see past the hood of the cab. My nerves became raw as I sat upright with my eyes on the road ahead.

"So this is how they protect you? By sticking you in a big cloud—"

"Shana Murphy. Um-hmm." My mother pressed her lips into a straight line. I saw a momentary flicker of rage on her face. My father leaned up to glare at me with furious emerald eyes.

Telling lies about my background was going to take a lot of practice.

"Um, driver, is it always like this in Noxhelm?"

"I don't know. This is my first time driving here, and my last. Fog and mountains shouldn't mix," he said as he slowed the car and sat up in his seat.

"Great."

My mother borrowed my phone and entered the address into the map. It was a good thing the miasma let up a bit by the time we arrived in our new neighborhood. The street sign said Misty Green Lane. The houses seemed nice but suburban. Not the expensive brownstone in the big city I had lived in— the houses we passed were large with yards. A pit formed in my stomach as we drove by a fenced yard with two dogs. I inhaled to fill my lungs, trying to force the thoughts of Hugo from my brain.

"What a cute area," my mother said. I could hear the apprehension in her voice.

We turned on Moorgate Street and searched for house number 203. I sat up, trying to view the house numbers. The home sizes had increased from Misty Green Lane, and I became a tad hopeful that things wouldn't be too terrible.

"Driver, right there. The big one on the right," my father said.

My eyes soaked in the sinister abode, labeled with a brass plate: number 203. The house was out of place, like the black sheep of the street.

"Hashtag nope. I'm not staying in that. What the hell?"

My mother cleared her throat and snapped her fingers. "Shana, that's enough. Not another word."

I had reached her tolerance level. The driver hopped out of the car to retrieve our luggage from the trunk, and we stayed in the back seat for an impromptu family meeting.

"Mother, that's a haunted house — people will be lining up to take a tour in October. What is that tiny circle window on top? An attic? Nope! Did they hide people up there, keep them prisoner? Torture them? Open your eyes. Look around. It doesn't belong on this street with all these nice brick houses with clean lawns and iron fences. We're supposed to be low key, right? That house stands out like, hello, psychos live here! Come and get us!"

"The marshals said they got a good deal, and the home is fully furnished. We are lucky to have this place. They usually set families up in a small place that they furnish with real cheap particle-wood stuff you have to put together."

"Why'd they get a good deal? I know! Because

the last people couldn't stand living there. Probably fled in the middle of the night, maybe got driven out by rats?"

My dad massaged his temples and spoke with a controlled tone. "Out of the car, now, and slap a smile on your face. If you don't want to be banished to the attic tonight, lose the attitude."

He swung open the door and climbed onto the sidewalk. Without a word, I followed his lead and grabbed my suitcase, facing the dreadful house on the hill. The pointed tips on the multilayer roof made it look even taller, and it was already at the highest point in the neighborhood. There was a long, cracked cement staircase that led to the front door.

"Wake up, Shana. You're just in a nightmare," I mumbled to myself as I climbed the steps.

Our house in Boston had been constructed in the early 1900s, but my parents had renovated it and hired an interior decorator that chose pristine, sterile white decor. This house may have been built the same year, but the pile of wood appeared to be in its original state with chipped siding and missing roof tiles. My dad opened the door, and a wave of sadness struck me when Hugo wasn't there to greet us. For the last ten years, our dog had burst out of the foyer to jump on me when I came home. I bit my quivering lip and walked inside, inhaling the musty air.

"Welcome home, Murphy family. They've stocked the fridge, and we've all got fresh sheets.

We've got seven bedrooms, so, Shana, take your pick. Other than the master suite," my dad said as we walked into the foyer.

The wood-paneled walls of the foyer darkened the space, and there was a zigzag staircase a few steps from the front door. I had hoped there would be a bedroom on the bottom floor, so I could be farthest from the attic. To my left was a floral-wallpapered living area with a low-hanging chandelier. The dark drapes, wood floors, and mahogany furniture were overwhelming. A red balloon floated in the center of the room, hovering about four feet above the ground without a string attached. When I took steps toward the piano, it glided in the same direction.

"Mom. What's with that balloon?"

My mother stared into the living area, and the balloon stilled. "A balloon? It's probably left over from an open house. Or maybe the feds left it as a housewarming token."

A housewarming token? Did she see the same thing I did? No ribbons, only enough helium to drift four feet above the ground. I backed out of the living room, and it floated toward me, slow and methodical. It didn't move like anything I'd seen before. My thoughts scrambled to understand how this thing mimicked me. Denying my fear, I set out to find a bedroom on the first floor by walking to the other side of the staircase and into the dining room.

"Get the hell back," I said as the balloon approached with far too steady of a movement to have been pushed by an air current.

My feet took a brisk walk through the dining room and into the adjoining parlor. A mournful, classical tune was playing on an old radio. If I had been trying to scare myself on purpose, I couldn't have done better with the wallpaper, couches, and drapes — all in the color of freshly spilled blood. The balloon stopped at the threshold and didn't move forward.

"You don't like the scary music, do ya?" I said. Sweeping my hand across my forehead, I got rid of the sweat.

"Shana, who are you talking to?" my father said from the adjacent room.

Realizing I had been taunting a balloon, I followed his voice to the kitchen.

"Mom finds nothing strange about a balloon escorting me around the house. Oh yeah, a gift from the feds. What the hell, are you joking? I want out of here, now!"

"Shana, stop being a drama queen. Shall we see what's here to eat?" she said.

The outdated room had maybe been nice in its day, with a turquoise refrigerator and a foldout table in the center of a blue vinyl floor with brown pleather chairs pushed underneath. The kitchen didn't fit in with the rest of the lavish decor of the house.

"Wow, how nice," I said with sarcasm riddling my tone.

"We can work with this. This tile's kinda cool,

huh?" my mother said as she glided her hands along the blue kitchen counter.

"Mother, that's shower tile. How tacky."

She opened the refrigerator and scanned the selection. I was certain the feds wouldn't know the first thing about what we would buy at the grocery store.

"How about breakfast for dinner? There are eggs, bacon, and I see some bread and butter. We're all set. You guys hungry?"

"I certainly am," my father said before he exited the room.

Deciding to stay with my mother to avoid the latex demon from hell, I sat at the table while she cooked. My dad had set off for a self-guided tour of the house.

The adrenaline in my veins had waned by the time dinner was ready. I hadn't had a full night's sleep since my life had been ripped away. I was dying to tell my story to Monica, my best friend, and I wondered what she was thinking about my sudden disappearance. I strained to remember her phone number, but after programming it into my phone when we were eleven, I hadn't viewed it since. I jumped when the doorbell rang.

"Were the marshals sending someone over?" my mother asked.

My dad scurried back into the kitchen, and my parents exchanged worried glances. I supposed this was how things would be for a while.

"I don't know. Stay here," my father said, then took off to answer the door.

My mother rummaged through a drawer, produced a steak knife, and held it by her side as she stood in the doorway of the kitchen.

"Mom, seriously? We're gonna do this every time someone comes over?"

The door creaked open, and my father's voice was calm, so she put the knife away and sat back down at the table with an enormous sigh. A young girl appeared with my dad in the kitchen. She had a swooping blue bang that hit her chin, and she wore dark lipstick. Pretty, but with obvious attempts at being alternative, as if she didn't care about her appearance but secretly tried her best.

"Shana, this is Andrea Clark from next door," my father said.

She grinned and waved with polished black nails filed into sharp points.

"May I be excused? I haven't picked out my room yet. Maybe Andrea can help me?"

"Sure," my mother said. "Nice to meet you, Andrea. You can call me Bronnie-Jo, and this is" — she hesitated for an awkward moment — "Ian. We're the Murphys, from Chicago."

I thought she was being too obvious. My mother was no actress.

"Come here — I want to show you something," I said as I marched into the red room. I wanted to show this girl the weird balloon, but when I got there, it was gone. For fear of her thinking I was crazy, I dropped the issue.

"Oh, sorry. I thought maybe this was a bedroom," I lied.

She was in awe, staring at the decor. "You know, I've never been in this house, but I've lived next to it for ten years. I know about this house, though," she said as her eyes darted around the room. "It's different."

"It certainly is." I laughed. "Do you mind helping me pick out my bedroom? I just find this place a bit peculiar and don't want to go upstairs alone. I mean, I'm not a chicken or anything, but it's been a long day—"

"I'd be glad to, Shana. Let's go pick your room."

Back at my private school, we all dressed the same with plaid skirts and navy blazers. We weren't allowed to wear T-shirts, or even polish our nails. Andrea had on a Slayer T-shirt, black leggings, and combat boots. I'd never met anyone like her before, but she seemed nice.

"I wonder how far this staircase goes?" I asked.

"It can't go too far—the house is only two stories," Andrea said.

With a creak on every step, we reached the first landing and turned the corner to go up the next flight.

"No, it's three stories counting the attic, which I find to be rather disturbing," I said.

"Yeah, I don't blame you, I hate attics."

We reached the top of the staircase and entered a long passage with a floral strip of carpet down the center. I flipped a switch, and sconces lit up along the wall. Bedroom doors lined both sides — four on the right and three on the left. Andrea opened the first door on the right and walked inside. It was majestic with a four-column poster bed and black paisley bedding.

"Master bedroom. Wow, this is pretty big. Has a fireplace," Andrea said.

"All right, my parents are here, so get me as far away as possible," I said with a laugh.

We walked down the hall and entered the third bedroom on the left. My lungs seized from the musty air. It was constricting, and I struggled for each breath.

"This was her room."

"Her room? She must have been ten, huh?"

The baby-pink walls with teen heartthrob posters on the wall were a bit much. I started to feel ill the longer I stood on the fluffy pink carpet. As I stepped back into the hallway, the red balloon caught my eye. It was by the staircase. My heart skipped a beat.

"Andrea, look."

"Um, why are you whispering?"

I nodded my head, looking down the hall, and she popped her head out just as the balloon descended the staircase.

"Dang." I sprinted down the carpet runner, but the balloon moved at a rapid pace down the stairs, as if it was trying to escape.

"Never mind, it was nothing." By the time she caught up, the thing had reached the corner of the landing and was sliding down the second flight. Emptiness took hold of my stomach. With quick breaths, I ran my fingers through my hair. "What were you saying about her—whose pink room was that?"

Andrea moved to the railing nonchalantly and peered down the stairs before she followed me back into the hall.

"Tragic story. She was a nice girl. Her name was Merry Biggs. She was thirteen, took some drugs, and lost her mind. The whole thing's very sad, and the dad was devastated and left Noxhelm."

"Drugs? At thirteen?"

"Some new type of drug. They call it Lapse or something like that. I stay away from that crap. Hope you do, as well." She gazed at me with a curious expression passing over her face.

"Certainly. Never touch the stuff." We approached the fourth door on the right. "Hey, what about this room?"

The door creaked as she opened it, and she shut it quickly. Junk was stacked floor to ceiling. "Maybe not this one."

The third room on the right had air that was easier to breathe. The decor was pleasing enough with a brass queen bed and dark-purple bedding. "Looks like a guest room. I'll take it." I checked the armoire—there was a television!

"I should warn you, since you picked a room on this side of the house."

She crept over to the window, and the hairs stood

up on my arms as my skin prickled.

"Oh, gosh. Do I need to move to the other side of the hall?" I took a step toward the door.

Andrea laughed. "No. But if you choose this room, I'll visit more—purely for entertainment. Come here."

The hardwood floor creaked with every step. She pulled back the drapes, and we fell into positions on either side of the window. The sun casted an eerie orange glow across the dimming sky. An old woman with wispy hair sat in a rocking chair surrounded by a patch of fog. There were creepy wind chimes hanging above her head. The porch was on the side of a small cottage, and just like the house we stood in, it didn't go with the rest of the brick homes in the cookie-cutter neighborhood. She held a basting brush and dipped it into a wooden bowl as she chanted something, but we couldn't make out the words through the window. She flung a clear substance toward my house, then stopped to gaze at me. I held back a scream and flattened myself against the wall out of her sight.

"Holy hell. She saw me, looked right in my eyes. Oh, my gosh. What are those things hanging above her head?"

Andrea bit her lips to hide a smile. Then she started laughing so loud it became soundless.

"No, seriously. This is the weirdest thing I've ever witnessed. What's going on with that lady?"

"Her name's Tabatha Gill. The wind chime things hanging from those chains are made of human teeth and hair—or at least that's what everyone says. She's always casting spells on everyone in the neighborhood."

"And nobody cares about that?"

Andrea plucked at her shirt to cool down and wiped a tear of laughter from her eye. "The HOA folks have met about her, but her house, and yours, are not technically part of Misty Oaks, so they're not ruled by the HOA. Kind of a glitch, you could say."

"HOA?"

"A neighborhood government that tells everyone what to do. I dunno. Well, I've got to get home; my mom was making dinner when I left. I just wanted to come over and say hi. I'm right next door if you need anything." She took steps toward the door and then stopped. "Oh, wanna walk to school with me tomorrow? I assume you're still in school, right? You're a junior, maybe a senior?"

"Senior."

"Wow, graduation's in three weeks!" Her eyes widened. "I'm a senior, too. Hope we have some classes together so I can help you." She shook her head with pinched brows. "Your parents couldn't hold off the move?"

I forced a smile on my face and hesitated with a nervous laugh. I hadn't planned on how to answer that question. "It's not like I had input. My dad moved here for work. Yes, come get me in the morning. I'm sure I won't sleep. I'll be up early—especially if ol' Tabatha keeps that up all night." I grabbed my phone from my pocket. "Oh, I don't know my number. This account is new. What's yours? I'll call you so you have mine."

We exchanged numbers as I escorted her down to the foyer and said goodbye. It was good to have a friend, but I couldn't stop the aching feeling of not speaking to Monica back in Boston.

I shouted toward the kitchen. "Mom, Dad, I'm in the third on the right. I'm not hungry. I'm going to try to get some sleep."

Exhausted, I figured I would collapse and pass out, so I sprang up the staircase. A few steps onto the floral runner of the hallway, I heard a banging noise from down the hall. I remained quiet, trying to determine the source. Another crash boomed as if someone had thrown something against the wall. My muscles tensed as the doorknob twisted on the last door on the left—Merry Biggs's room. I opened my mouth to speak, but nothing came out. I was paralyzed. The knob shot back into position, and everything fell silent. To preserve my sanity, I convinced myself I had imagined it as a result of stress and lack of sleep. With trembling limbs, I hurried into my bedroom and slammed the door behind me.

The moon had emerged in the hazy sky. With cautious steps, I stormed across the room and shut my drapes without looking to see if the old woman was still casting spells on my house. Fumbling through my suitcase, I found a great set of yellow Minion pajamas. The feds must have had good profilers to pack such a suitcase, figuring out that

Despicable Me was my favorite movie. I climbed into bed and opened the Yipper app on my phone. I didn't log in to my account, but I wanted to see what my friends had said about my disappearance. As expected, Monica had posted a long note filled with confusion and sadness. Somehow she had learned my father had purchased another gun range in Mexico, and we had moved to a remote location with no Wi-Fi or towers to get a phone signal. I wondered who had made up that tall tale, and why she would have believed such an absurd story.

A text message made my phone vibrate, and my heart fluttered. I hadn't given out the number to anyone besides Andrea, and the message was from an unknown number. I clicked on it, and it was a photo of my new house with the caption, I see you. I brushed it off and forced myself to sleep.

7-THE NEW KID

The following morning, I awoke in soaked sheets, panting for air. Moments before, I had been standing in the fog in front of my house on the concrete steps with a young blonde girl on the sidewalk. Her messy hair was tied with a red satin ribbon that matched her frilly shirt. Her eyes streamed blood down her porcelain cheeks as she pointed toward my house. I tried to talk to her, ask her what was wrong, but she twisted her body in the direction of Tabatha's house and released an earsplitting scream. I hadn't endured such a vivid nightmare since I was a child. The room was dark with a sliver of sunlight streaming through the drapes. I slid out of bed, walked over, and pulled them open. The sun had barely risen, and fog surrounded the window. My brain threw me back to the clouds on the plane, waiting for the next violent bout of turbulence. I shook off the feeling and peered at the clock on the wall, hoping it was set to the right time. It read 6:14 a.m. There was plenty of time to sort through the luggage to see if there was anything acceptable to pass off as my wardrobe for the day. A baby-blue oxford shirt and khaki pants caught my eye, both the correct size. I checked the toiletry bag, and there was a straightener and close to the same products I used to get ready. I continued to be impressed with the profiler who had packed my bag.

The shower was hot, pressure was moderate, and the counter was big enough for all my stuff. Once I was ready, I crept down the hallway. My mother's voice resonated from their bedroom.

"I cannot believe you kept a phone. Cullen, I mean Ian, that's stupid! They can be tracked, you know. You want Vince sending a guy over again? You don't even have a gun here—how will we protect ourselves?"

"It's not like I had time to grab a gun last time. I was blindsided, but we managed. But I'm going to open a gun range here. I have three months to start earning a legit living."

"I thought they gave you enough money for six months?"

"You want to live like a pauper for that long? Give me a break, Courtney. I had to talk to Mickey to get the numbers of my vendors and stuff."

"Are you serious? You're going to use your vendors? They all know you. They know Vince. Are you trying to get caught?"

I had planned to talk to my parents about the strange text I had received the night before, but they were otherwise engaged. The feds had worked out my transfer to the new school. My parents had given me the option of starting in the morning or waiting another day, and I wanted to get out and meet people. I left a note in the foyer for them.

After waiting a few seconds on my foggy front porch, I realized the humidity was going to curl my hair, so I went back inside. I feared what walking to school would do, but maybe I wouldn't earn the same horrible nicknames with this group of kids if I did sprout a few ringlets. I exhaled when Andrea knocked on the door. I shouted that I was leaving, and my mother yelled back, promising a shopping trip for clothes later. That put a smile on my face.

I stepped outside. "Hey, girl. So, tell me—is everyone pretty cool?"

She smirked. "Not exactly. Lots of interesting personalities."

"Great. I suppose I can stomach anything for a few weeks. How long's the walk?"

"Three blocks down Misty Green Lane and the school's on Willenhall Way."

We made our way down the steps and onto the sidewalk, turning the opposite direction of the old woman's house. I paused to snap a photo of my house surrounded by fog. My old friends would never believe we lived in such a place if I didn't have proof.

"Do you have a boyfriend?" I asked.

"You could say that, but we haven't gone public yet."

A car engine hummed in the distance. The car

emerged from the fog, passing us on the street.

"Is it foggy every day? Doesn't it get annoying?"

"It's here about three-fourths of the year. Typically burns off midday, though. You get used to it, and I bet you'll like the advantages."

"Such as?"

We waited for the crossing guard at Falcon Street.

"You can get away with stuff if you need to," she said with a laugh.

"Oh yeah. Did you text me last night, maybe from another phone or something?"

"Nope, I haven't texted you yet, but I'll try during art history. I do everything I can to keep my eyes open. I've even gone live on Yipper and made funny faces the whole time to stay awake."

My stomach hardened for a moment as my brain analyzed the photo from the unknown number. The only other person who may have known my new cell number was Mr. Doyle. Deep down, I knew Mr. Doyle would never have sent that message. Something wasn't adding up, but I didn't feel that I was in imminent danger, so I put it at the back of my mind once again.

"Come here," an elderly voice said from behind us.

Andrea tugged on my sleeve for me to continue walking. Curious, I made an instant decision to turn around. The old woman locked eyes with me. It was Tabatha Gill.

"Have you seen Merry Biggs? In the house, have you seen her?" she asked me.

Befuddled, I exchanged glances with Andrea, and she shrugged a shoulder, trying to erase the smirk on her face. The old woman caught up, stepping into my intimate space, so I backed up.

"Ma'am, she doesn't live there anymore. Something happened to her, but I don't know the details. Maybe do an online search or something," I said.

Tabatha gawked at me with little black beads for eyes surrounded by puffy bags of skin that fell onto her cheeks. She had a corpselike complexion, and her teeth didn't extend past her pleated lips, giving the sense she was either toothless or wearing a worn set of dentures.

"Merry's the only one who speaks to my daughter, Violet. I'd like to speak to Violet."

"Um, does she go to Noxhelm High?" Andrea said.

Tabatha's eyes burned into me as she stood still without saying a word.

"All right, take care, Ms. Gill." Andrea grabbed my arm as the guard signaled for us to cross the street.

"She's nuts," I whispered.

"Told you."

About half of a block later, we merged with a crowd of students walking toward the school. Andrea introduced me to a few people, but it was difficult to remember all of their names, especially since they were looking at me as if I were an alien. I guessed they hadn't had many new kids, given the location and size of the town. Andrea escorted me to the front office and then zipped down the hall. I was all set to go for my first day. After visiting with a counselor to discuss what I had to do for graduation, I set off to find my first class with a queasy stomach.

"New kid, huh? I heard we'd have one today," a middle-aged ginger-haired lady said; she wore bright-red lipstick and a fifties-style dress. "My name is Ms. Hayes, and this is English Literature. We are currently studying In Cold Blood by Truman Capote."

I'd read the novel in tenth grade, so I smiled.

"Great. Do I just pick a seat?" My voice was shaky.

"Sit anywhere you'd like."

The kids in the class stared at me, and my heart started palpitating. I exhaled as I spied an empty spot next to Andrea at the back of the classroom. We traded smiles as I dropped into the seat. The teacher was engaging and kept the class alive. Before I knew it, the bell rang.

After a monotone statistics class, I entered physiology as the new kid once again, and found a seat. The girl beside me cocked her head to the side and glared with brilliant blue eyes behind wire-framed glasses. She had a short, wavy bob, nearly the same shade as mine but not as intense. It was May, but she was wearing what resembled the sheepskin rug that Maurice Flynn had bled on back in my Boston living room. I supposed she wore the thing for fashion's sake, but she should have left it in the closet, or better yet — used it as a rug.

"Hello, my name is — "

"Shana Murphy, I know." She slammed her book closed, pushed back in her chair, and crossed her arms. She turned to gaze out the window.

"Excuse me — did I do something to you?"

Across the aisle, the nerdy guy I recognized from the plane stood from his chair and approached.

"Jackie, you should be nice to the new girl."

"Shut up, Don. You know why I'm pissed."

In an utter state of confusion, I sat in silence, waiting for one of them to blurt out a clue about what I'd done.

"Hey, Lynda."

Jackie's mood lightened as a girl with bushy hair approached. She wore a sweater so neon yellow, it hurt my eyes.

"What's going on here, guys? Hello, Don, I see you haven't got your cast off yet," Lynda said.

The nerdy guy raised his arm to show off his cast. It had only a couple of signatures on it. "I get it off later this evening. It's been difficult to live without my dominant hand, that's for sure."

"Didn't you break it during a fight with your brother?"

"Stepbrother and yes."

The teacher shot a foul look in our direction and then shouted for us all to take our seats. What followed was another annoying welcome speech for the new kid. I hated being a spectacle. The class dragged on as I sat by the hostile girl, who scowled at me the whole time. At one point, the teacher stopped class to ask if there was a problem, but we both said no.

Lunch followed, and I was glad to find Andrea. By the time we made it through the long line, we had five minutes to cram the subpar food down our throats. I couldn't find the right moment without being overheard to ask her about my newfound archenemy from physiology. A girl with a colorful scarf around her head approached our table from behind.

"Oh, look, it's the new girl with the bright-orange hair." I turned toward her. "And ew — her eyes are green like snot." She let out a jarring laugh. "I don't see what's so special about her, do you, Lynda?" The bushy-haired girl from physiology with the neon sweater stood by her side.

"Come on, Stephanie. Don't do this," Lynda said.

Andrea's eyes widened, and her mouth gaped open. She was as confused as me.

"Oh, I'm gonna do this. Lynda, back off."

I turned my head as Stephanie stepped toward me until her kneecap grazed my back. Turning forward, I widened my eyes at Andrea, clenching my fists until my knuckles turned white.

"What's your problem? What have I possibly done to you?" I said through tight lips without turning around. I stayed in my seat with my eyes forward. The O'Sullivan gene had been triggered, and a heat wave rushed through my core, my hands tingling. A table of girls in front of me slowly turned their heads to eavesdrop on what was happening at my table.

Stephanie leaned down and spoke loudly in my ear. "Ha! You exist, Shana Murphy. What you've done to make me hate you is exist."

Andrea slammed her hand on the table. "Stephanie, back off. Just stop."

"Oh, wow. The Goth girl's got your back, Snot Eyes. How charming."

With tunnel vision and grinding teeth, I stood and faced her. The next words that spewed from my mouth were beyond my control and garnered unwanted attention. "I haven't done anything to anybody in this dumb school or this godforsaken town, so you and all your stupid friends who hate me for no good reason can go to hell!"

As soon as the last word flew from my tongue, I spotted my physiology teacher on lunchroom patrol. She was walking toward us with a scowl on her face. A small crowd had gathered with a few phones in the air, recording the exchange. Girls were giggling, and a few boys were egging us on. Since this was the second time the teacher had witnessed me in turmoil, I paused, waiting for her to send me to the office. She gave me a blank stare. Stephanie noticed the teacher, pushed her way through the group of spectators, and stormed out of the cafeteria as the bell rang.

"Man, I don't know what's wrong with her, but I'll try to find out for you, Shana." Andrea said. "I'm sorry, but I have to run."

We put our trays up and parted ways once we got in the hallway. Lynda pulled me to the side.

"Shana, I'm sorry about my friends' behavior. No excuse, but we're not used to having new students at school, especially not pretty ones who get attention. They're just in shock and exuding a bit of jealously from what all the guys have been saying. It will subside."

"I guess I should be flattered?" I asked.

She laughed and tapped me on the shoulder. "Yes, you could say that. You've definitely caught one guy's attention, that's for sure."

Before I could ask her what she was talking about, she rushed off. My mind deliberated during the next period about the mystery guy, but since I knew no one, it didn't matter. After a snooze fest in art history, I forged on to advanced health, my final class of the day. I dreaded another teacher's monologue about welcoming the new kid.

"Hey, I know you!" a male voice yelled from the middle of the classroom as I stepped across the threshold.

I glanced around the room, unsure if the voice was directed at me. The guy I'd sat next to on the plane to California was smiling at me, pointing at an empty chair. Bowing my head, I recalled my behavior once the turbulence had taken over the flight. I had been so nervous, everything had turned into a blur, and I'm sure he thought I was rude. By the time we had landed, I'd rushed off the plane, buzzing with excited nerves.

"Blaine Walker, right?" I said as I slipped into the desk beside him.

"At least you remember my name." He chuckled. "So, we meet again. I heard about you starting school today. It's a small town, so get used to it."

"I was going to say—news spreads quickly, huh?"

"But listen, I'm having a big Cinco de Mayo fiesta at my casa on Friday. I'd love it if you could come."

"Oh, I'd love to, but after today, I think I should—"

"I already know about Jackie. She's my ex and a little jealous of you."

"Of me? Why? I don't understand."

"Come on, Shana. Don't be bashful. You're beautiful. She feels threatened. But Stephanie's another story—she's just a flat-out psychopath." He laughed. "But I've already had people talk to them, and neither will come to my party if they don't apologize. We're adults, or some of us are, and we shouldn't act like children."

"What about Andrea Clark? Um, do you know her? Is she invited?"

He shook his head. "She's not invited, so please don't mention anything to her about it." He cleared his throat.

"Why is she not invited?"

"She just doesn't get along with anyone, and I don't want drama." He smiled. "So, I live on the other side of the crazy witch lady—the one next to you. My house is on the corner, facing Romford Drive. Just walk on over whenever you can, okay?"

I closed my eyes and took a calming breath. "I'll see what my parents say."

"You still listen to your parents? How cute."

He squeezed my knee as he laughed. I got the feeling he liked me and had maybe even said something to Jackie about me that had made her mad. I didn't want to betray my only friend on my first day, so I didn't know what I was going to do. The teacher got our attention by banging a steel apple on her desk.

"Today, we are going to be discussing a drug that has infected our town within the last year. I'm talking about Lapse—an extremely dangerous opioid compound that also contains a hallucinogen that when consumed can have deadly consequences. You may have heard of it." The students mumbled, pointing at each other and snickering. "When taken, the drug switches off parts of the cerebral cortex—the section of your brain for problem solving, emotion, and complex thought. The result is a primal shell, a primitive version of yourself who will act on impulse alone. For this reason, it can be a lethal drug. We will be doing random sweeps of areas of the campus over the next week. Today, this classroom has been selected for a sweep, so everyone empty your pockets and place your things on your desktops. Leave your backpacks on the floor by your desks, and follow me outside. The police dogs are coming in to sniff the aromas in here.

It won't take the police long to do their job."

Blaine slipped his hand into his backpack, pulled out a pencil case, and slipped it into the back of his pants as we lined up for inspection. We were asked to pull out our pocket liners as we walked through the door. What was he hiding from the police search?

After school, just as Andrea and I took off down the sidewalk, Blaine pulled up next to us in his convertible BMW. He said to hop in, and he'd take us home. Without hesitation, Andrea climbed in the front seat as if they were friends. I was puzzled how both of them could be in chipper moods while around each other, yet he still hadn't invited her to his party. I had planned to speak to Andrea about Blaine's behavior during the drug sweep. I wasn't the type of person to rat on anyone, but being new to town, I wanted to know the people I would be around.

The fog had nearly vanished, and the town became visible. I could understand why the marshal had said the place was charming, as everything was neatly built with street signs hanging from decorative poles. Uniform hedges lined the main thoroughfare of Misty Green Lane. The homes had well-manicured lawns with overflowing flower gardens lining their front porches. As we passed by, it was surreal, as though we were driving through a page in Beautiful Garden magazine. In less than three minutes, Blaine parked the car in between our houses on Moorgate Street and said goodbye.

As I climbed the steps to my front door, my phone vibrated. Andrea had already gone inside, but I assumed it was her, as she had promised to text earlier. It was from an unknown number—a photo of Andrea and me in the car with Blaine. The caption said, Why did you ride with him?

8-CINCO DE MAYO

The alarm on my phone blasted at 6:00 a.m. on Friday, but I didn't feel rested. Overwhelmed, I was desperate for a genuine conversation with my mother, as we hadn't talked about things since Boston, and I had no one else. Without a restful night in three days, an emotional breakdown was looming. The night before, my parents had ordered a pizza for me and left the house for dinner. They had done nothing but bicker since we had arrived in Noxhelm. I assumed they had gone out to give me a break, but they weren't doing me any favors because their incessant debates were far better than being alone in that house. My mother had slipped a sleeping pill on my nightstand with a note for me to get to bed early. It still took more than an hour of me hiding under the covers for me to fall asleep to creaking boards and clatters. My parents had explained that old houses just made noise, but I didn't agree with their rationalization.

I slid out of bed and set out to find my mother,

pausing by the master suite door. I quieted my breathing, pressing my ear to the door. Silence. Thinking she was in the kitchen, my feet took the steps with haste.

"Shana, come here," a young girl's voice said from downstairs. I slowed my pace on the second flight.

As both feet landed on the hard wood of the foyer, my eyes shot to the red balloon hovering above the ground in the living room. A flush of adrenaline tingled through my body. My posture stiffened, muscles turned rigid. The latex demon had suddenly appeared to gain weight, and it bounced, struggling to stay afloat. A sorrowful melody switched on in the parlor from the old radio. As I planned a quick escape, my hand felt backward for the stair railing, but I never took my eyes off the balloon as it drifted slowly toward me. An opaque liquid dripped from its knot, making a trail below.

"Mom? Are you in the kitchen?"

It halted after I spoke, as if it waited to see if she would respond. The parlor music's volume amplified. The evil thing moved in my direction, gaining velocity as the volume pumped higher, as if the song fueled the movement. The liquid poured from the knot and pooled on the floor. Suddenly, the radio went silent.

"Shana, come here." The girl's voice echoed from the parlor.

With a full body tremble, I slid along the rail en route to the staircase, but the balloon blocked my path. The liquid oozing onto the ground was a deep crimson. The warm puddle spread to my toes, and I detected a faint aroma of copper. It was blood.

"Mom! Dad!"

Just as I shouted, the pitter-patter of bare footsteps sounded from the dining room, and the music switched back on. It had changed to a funeral hymn. I gripped the railing, heaving for my next breath of air with tears gushing down my cheeks.

"Shana, I need your help." The girl's voice grew closer, sounding almost inhuman as it faded out.

"Leave me alone!"

With an earsplitting pop, the balloon exploded, and blood splattered everywhere, coating the walls, the stairs, everything. A primal scream left my lungs as I covered my blood-streaked face with my hands and plastered my body against the rail, sobbing. I dropped down into a fetal position with my head between my knees as a voice called my name repeatedly.

"Shana!" My mother's voice rang out in the distance. I screamed until her hands grabbed my shoulders, and the funeral hymn faded away. I wheezed for air as I opened my eyes, the light burning my retina as I swallowed hard lumps. "Shana! Wake up!"

In my bed, I braced myself on my elbows, eyes darting around my room as I squinted. My pajamas were drenched, but it was sweat, not blood. "Mom, it was terrible." I threw my arms around her and wept. "I just want to go home. This place is a nightmare. Everything about this town is wrong."

She pulled me in for a tighter hug and rubbed my back.

"It was a nightmare, honey. You're fine, I promise." She stayed in place until I stopped bawling; then she backed her head off my shoulder to gaze at me. "All right, the Noxhelm High counselor gave us a call yesterday. She said you needed to stop by after school on Monday for a session. They understand moving can be taxing on young people, and they mentioned you were fighting with some folks at school."

I escaped her embrace and narrowed my eyes at her. "Ugh, a couple of girls were just mean! I didn't start it."

"Honey, I know. That's okay, and it's all to be expected. You're going through a lot right now, more than girls your age should have to endure. If you need to take time off school, Dad and I will stand behind your decision. You haven't been accepted for your top college choices for the fall, so we have to submit another round of applications, anyway. I don't think a summer graduation will hurt you one bit. Maybe you can pick up some classes in community college?"

I sighed, pulling my shirt back and forth from my body to dry it. The last thing I wanted to do was talk about college.

"Don't minimize what I've been dealing with, please. Yes, the school's terrible. True—I'm having nightmares, and I'm stressed. Maybe I've even been hearing things in this creepy house, or whatever. But one thing you cannot deny is that someone is playing games." I grabbed my phone from the nightstand and opened the text thread.

She studied the photos from the unknown number. "Too bad we're on the outs with Vince. He's got a guy who could trace this in two seconds." She shook her head. "But don't worry, honey. This seems more like a sick high school prankster just trying to get to you because you're new here. Have you given your phone number out?"

"Just to the neighbor, Andrea."

"Then it's her!"

"Mom, she's in one of the pictures, so how could it be?"

"She gave your number to someone who did. Kids are mean. Even back home, you had your share of troubles."

I shrugged my shoulders. She was right, but the difference was that in Boston, my father would have taken care of any of my problems with one phone call.

"So what's going on between you and Dad? I hear you guys arguing, you know."

"The move's been stressful. Your father isn't adjusting well to the sudden change. He keeps trying to build the same life here, in this town, while we're undercover. I'm just afraid we'll be discovered."

"Has he told anyone where we are?"

"Not sure, but he's kept in touch with Mickey

Doyle. I trust Mick, but not John Patrick. Your father's being irrational."

I wasn't sure what I could say, as I loved both of my parents and didn't want to pick a side.

"I was invited to a Mexican fiesta party, and it's tonight. A boy's house, on the other side of that crazy lady."

"Crazy lady?"

"You haven't see her? There's an old hag next door who performs spells under a wind chime of human teeth and hair. Mom, she's in that wood cabin shack thing with the patio that faces us. She is terrifying."

My mother cackled. "Oh, Shana the drama queen with the vivid imagination. How I love you, let me count the ways. You have got to be a writer one day, as your debut will be a bestseller."

"Okay, woman. You'll see. Hope she comes over to borrow some sugar, and a lock of hair, and one of your molars."

We both fell about laughing for a moment. My mother quieted when my father strolled into my room.

"Hey, sunshine. You're up with the roosters — crowing with them, too. I heard you screaming. Nightmare, I presume?"

She climbed off my bed and marched out of my bedroom without a word. He paused as she passed by. This wasn't good.

"Yes, it was a bad one." I shrugged.

"You doing okay, otherwise, sweetheart? I'm so

sorry — this must be devastating."

"Um, given the circumstances, I'm doing fine. I've seen better days, for sure."

"I'll get you home as soon as I can. I promise." He leaned in and gave me a tight hug and kissed my forehead. "I love you, Shana. You're my world."

"Love you, too, Daddy. Hey, can I ask you something?"

"Sure, of course," he said with a smile.

"A boy invited me to a party tonight. He said the Goth chick next door isn't invited. Should I go? I mean, Andrea's the only friend I have. But if I go, I may make more friends with people who are more like me. It's not like I've been welcomed here. I'm confused about what to do."

He grinned and patted me on the shoulder. "Go to the party. You know I've never been one to support any dealings with boys, but you've gotta get out there to make this place bearable until we go home. The counselor says you got into a few brawls at school on your first day?"

"Not exactly brawls, Dad. A couple of people were mean, but I think that's all okay now."

"Don't miss that party, and never let people get the best of you. You're an O'Sullivan. Wear the name proudly — even if you're in disguise for now." The doorbell rang, and my father hurried out of my bedroom. "I'll get it."

I jumped in the shower, hoping that it wasn't Andrea arriving early. After rushing through my hair and makeup, I sorted through three more days of clothes. Mom and I hadn't gone shopping as planned. Not wanting to reenact my nightmare, I hesitated at the top of the stairs before going down at top speed. In the living room, my father was sitting with Mickey Doyle, his best friend from Boston. I rushed over and gave Mr. Doyle a huge hug. After picking up faint footsteps from the dining room, I jogged over to investigate. My mother was pacing back and forth around the table with one arm wrapped around her waist, and the other crossing her chest and clenching her shoulder.

"Mom," I whispered. "What's going on?"

She took me by the hand and pulled me into the parlor. I gazed at the radio for a moment as we sat on the red couches, and a chill shuddered down my spine.

"He's told Mickey where we lived. We're all doomed."

"But it's Mr. Doyle. He's been Dad's friend since they were kids. Great-Grandpa raised him after his parents were wiped out in a car crash. He would never hurt us."

"I think they're both blinded by John Patrick. I think John's loyal to Vince and is using Mick to get information."

The doorbell rang again. Believing it was Andrea, I rushed to the door and swung it open. I swallowed a hard knot in my throat as the old woman from next door stepped up to me holding a basket of brownies. There was a blanket of sunny fog behind her.

"Good morning. May I come in?" she crooned.

My mother walked up behind me. "Hello, and you are?"

"Hello. My name is Tabatha Gill. I live next door and was stopping by to say hello and introduce myself. I brought you some treats I baked myself. May I please come in?"

I spun around to my mother and whispered, "No, do not let her in."

My mom put on a fake smile. "Certainly. Would you like some coffee?" She swung the door open wide and gestured for the witch to enter.

My insides quivered and stomach churned. Would she chant a bad luck hex, or was there a gun hidden in her basket? I glued my eyes to her, waiting for her to make a move. My mother escorted Ms. Gill through the living room, stopping to introduce her to my father before she disappeared into the kitchen. I followed, widening my eyes at my dad and Mr. Doyle along the way.

"I'm so glad you stopped by, Tabatha. I've been here a couple of days and haven't met a neighbor yet! These look delicious, thank you."

I pleaded in my head with her not to eat what the crazy lady had brought over, but she opened the cupboard and brought out three plates and coffee mugs.

"How do you take your coffee?"

"Black. Oh, I don't need a plate. I can't have sugar, but I just love making them and watching others enjoy themselves."

Of course she wouldn't eat one if they were poisoned.

"Would you like a cup, Shana?"

"No."

Pretending to browse on my phone, I sneaked a photo of Tabatha, as I'd have to tell this story when I got back to Boston. The doorbell rang once again.

"Mom, I don't mean to be rude, but you promised to walk with me to school. We have to go. Now." I said anything I could to get Tabatha out of my house and for my mother not to eat what she had brought over.

She grinned as she filled two mugs and placed a chocolate square of poison on a plate. "Don't be silly. You're almost eighteen and can walk with Andrea to school. I'm going to enjoy my morning coffee and one of Tabatha's delicious brownies. Have a great day, sweetheart."

9-THE HOUSEGUEST

With my mother weighing on my mind, I pushed off into the hallway at school. As English literature began, Andrea confessed to handing over my number to Jackie and Stephanie in the restroom before class. Ten minutes into the teacher's discussion of how the author had disclosed who had murdered the family at the start of the novel but kept the motives and connection reveal for the end, I received two text messages—both were short, contrived apologies. During physiology, Jackie was mechanical and didn't acknowledge that she had sent a text, but Lynda offered a sincere smile and waved hello. Don walked into class late and avoided eye contact—odd behavior, but I hadn't been friends with many nerds before, so I shrugged it off. At lunch, Andrea and I sat together once again, but I didn't see Stephanie, which was a good thing as far as I was concerned.

"Oh, I forgot to tell you this morning. Guess who stopped by."

"Well, I saw some man walk up the steps to your house. Who was that, I've never seen him before?"

"Ah, that's just my dad's friend. I'm talking about another unexpected guest."

She studied my eyes. "No way, Tabatha came over?"

I laughed. "Yes. And, she brought brownies. My mom invited her in and was about to eat one when you came over."

"Did she eat it?"

"Dunno. I hope not!"

"You should text her to see if she's okay!"

I sent a quick message. My mother replied within a minute with a sneaked photo of Tabatha sitting at the kitchen table with a coffee mug in her hands. I saved it onto my camera roll. That old woman had been in my house for hours. My poor mother.

"At least your mom's okay." Andrea laughed as the bell blasted, ending lunch.

I suffered through my lackluster afternoon classes until advanced health, where Blaine greeted me with a roguish grin, soaring my spirits high into the sky.

"Will I see you tonight, beautiful?"

After a few seconds of bathing in his charm, I responded. "Sure, I'll be there."

For the remainder of the class, the teacher's words faded off in the distance. Thoughts of Blaine's party dominated my thoughts until the bell rang and I met Andrea in the hallway.

"I just had a great idea," she said as we marched

through the front door and into the afternoon mist.

"What's that?"

"Let me save you from your house, now that Tabatha has cast spells all in it. For all you know, she's still there, talking your mom's ear off! Come over and spend the night!"

We laughed for nearly a block, joking about Tabatha moving in and becoming our roommate. Then Blaine's enchanting smile popped into my head.

"You know, Saturday would work best for me. My parents and I haven't had much time together since we moved here. They wanted to eat dinner with me and watch a movie."

"You'd rather hang out with your parents? Shana, come on—we can sneak over and knock on Tabatha's door and film her on a live Yipper feed when she comes out throwing witch juice in the air. How funny will that be?"

Her proposal sounded fun, but I had an overwhelming urge to go to the party.

"Can't we do that Saturday? I'll come over at noon, and we'll have all day to plan our attack on Tabatha."

"Oh, all right. Girl, you have all night to come up with something genius to do to her. Maybe research online for some counterspells?"

"That's a promise."

We approached our houses and said goodbye. A black Cadillac Escalade with darkly tinted windows crawled by as I stood watching from the sidewalk.

After it had disappeared down the street, I took the steps at a run and pushed open the front door. It wasn't locked, so I figured at least one of my parents were home. A note on the foyer desk said that they were out shopping and then headed to dinner. My dad had added a line at the bottom for me to have fun at the party.

Gloomy dread overcame me as I stared into the quiet, dark house that had terrorized me for three days. I rushed into the kitchen to grab a soda, passing by the half-empty basket of Tabatha's brownies. Why my parents would eat anything made by a lady with human teeth and hair hanging from chains on her patio was beyond my comprehension. Footsteps creaked on the staircase, and I paused with my finger on the soda tab.

"Mom? Dad? You home?"

I failed to get a response, but the ceiling creaked above me as if someone was walking down the upstairs hall. A big fan of horror flicks, I was aware the dumb girl always runs straight into danger and gets slashed, but it was the light of day, and curiosity surpassed my fear. I slid my soda on the table and tiptoed upstairs. A rush of cold air struck me as I crept across the carpet runner of the hallway. With goose bumps on my skin, I scanned the ceiling, but I couldn't find the antagonistic air vent. Merry's bedroom door swung slightly ajar. Holding my phone in front of me, I started recording a video as I walked toward the room. With each step closer, voices grew more distinct, and it became apparent that an elderly woman and a young girl were having a conversation.

My mind flew straight to a home invasion. "This is Shana Murphy. I live here. I'm calling the police right now."

I stood outside Merry's room, waiting for someone to come out, but it fell silent. After waiting a few minutes in the hall, I entered her room. The stuffy air grew thick in my lungs as I stepped onto the pink carpet. I could no longer hear the voices. On the opposing side of the room, there was a closet door. It was closed. I turned on my phone's flashlight, grabbed the closet door's knob, and opened it with an abrupt motion. I shivered as I took in Merry's wardrobe, color coordinated and hanging neatly on satin hangers. My feet twisted back around, and I crept toward a waist-high door next to the bed. With great caution, I pulled it open and shined the light across the threshold. A wooden staircase was illuminated. I figured it led to the attic.

"Anybody up there? Come on down. I've called the police. You should leave before they get here."

Feeling bold, I climbed the steps and up to the planks of the floor. The warm, stuffy air coated my lungs and reeked of mildew. Pink insulation filled rectangular crevices on either side of the room, and there was a single rocking chair in the middle of the space. Dust particles danced in the light stream bursting in through the circular window in the front. I spun around and faced Tabatha Gill, standing by the back window. Her arms were crossed, and she turned her head slowly to lock eyes with me.

"Oh, I apologize for startling you, dear. I just had to speak with Merry. She's the only one who my daughter, Violet, talks to, and I haven't heard from her in ages."

"Ms. Gill, please leave. Merry doesn't live here anymore, and as you can see, she's not here, so go."

The woman smiled, revealing an array of missing teeth and decay inside her mouth. It could have been the poorly mixed light of the attic, but her dark irises appeared to spread onto the whites of her eyes before bouncing back to their normal shape. My bag of candy from Boston caught my eye. It was behind a board in the corner of the attic. She was hiding it from me.

"You took my candy?" I stormed over, crossing a wooden plank that was suspended over a sea of pink chunks of insulation. "Ugh, you were in my room! Why?"

"Your mother gave me an open invitation, dear. I just popped over because Merry waved at me through the window as I was taking my afternoon stroll." Her bony finger pointed to the circular window at the front wall.

"But you stole my candy from my room. That's an invasion of privacy! You're a thief!"

Her irises oscillated again, and I stepped back toward the stairs, my stomach rock hard.

"Dear, I did no such thing."

"Please leave, before the police arrive."

My limbs grew shaky, and beads of sweat formed

on my forehead. She brushed by me and climbed down the stairs, and I followed. She slowed her pace through Merry's former bedroom, dragging her hand along the wall.

"I'll walk you to the front door, ma'am." I encouraged her to follow me as I entered the hallway. I stopped the recording on my phone. I would bring up the discussion of filing for a restraining order when I shared the video with my parents later. It grew easier to catch a breath after another patch of chilled air blew against my skin, but again, I couldn't find the vent.

"Merry told me to come back later. She said you were leaving for a party."

Blood rushed to my face. "She did not tell you that, Ms. Gill. You read that I was going to a party on the note my parents left me. Please do not enter our home when we are not here. It's illegal."

After a painstaking slow climb down the two flights of stairs, we entered the foyer, and I opened the front door.

"Have a nice time at the celebration, Shana. Merry said she would be there, so be cautious."

I cocked my head to the side. "Merry's going to the party?"

"No, not Merry. Another girl." She smiled. "Not a very nice girl."

Tabatha ambled out onto the front porch.

"What girl?"

"You should keep your wits about you, Shana Murphy," she said as she hobbled into the fog.

10-DEAD MAN'S PARTY

Trying to keep thoughts of Tabatha Gill out of my head, I took my time and made sure every hair was shiny and lying straight. I missed my closet with its racks of cute tops, but I sifted through what I had left in the suitcase. Green tank top and jeans. Fine. It was a Mexican fiesta, and green was a color on the flag, and it happened to be my best color.

My phone vibrated with a text from an unknown number. I deliberated whether to check the message, but my curiosity won out. It was a photograph of me through my bedroom window putting on the tank top with the caption, Green looks great on you, see ya soon.

I lunged for my window, grabbed the drapes, and yanked them shut. My candy from Boston was flat and melted from the attic heat. I threw the bag on the floor and held back tears to avoid messing up my eye makeup. I fought strong urges to log in to my accounts on Yipper and other platforms to chat with Monica. Playing scenarios of a quick trial for Vince, and a huge welcome-home party with all my friends back home, I found the courage to continue applying my makeup. I had two choices—stay in a creepy house by myself or be with people.

Unsure of what I would say if Andrea caught me sneaking toward the party, I marched out the front door and down the steps. She was right about the fog—it could serve a purpose. I was out of her range of sight after a brisk stroll down the sidewalk. I jogged past Tabatha's house, being careful not to break a sweat. Blaine's house was enormous with a contemporary, sharp-edge, multilevel design. The party buzzed with laughter and splashes in the swimming pool as I passed by the backyard. I knocked, and within seconds, Blaine swung open the thick glass front door.

"Hello, beautiful. Please come inside."

He held out his hand, and I gave him mine. He swept me through the foyer and past an elaborate bar. The backyard was stunning with an infinity pool surrounded by a jungle of beautiful plants and trees. We descended the steps to the swimming pool area, and I recognized a few faces from school.

"Can I grab you something to drink?" he said, as he dropped a Godiva chocolate into my hand.

I loved chocolate, so I didn't waste time before I opened it and popped it into my mouth. "You have Dr Pepper?"

"We have beer, you know."

"No, thank you. I don't drink." With an Irish father with a bad temper, I didn't dare do anything stupid like that.

"Dr Pepper it is," he said with a smile.

Blaine set off to get me a soda. I snapped a couple of photos of the people having fun in the pool, and then I stepped over to take one of the back of the house, for it was incredible with sharp roof lines and glass walls. Jackie stormed over with Stephanie, who had a bright scarf tied around her head and huge hoop earrings. Both girls wore skimpy bikinis and more makeup than all the Kardashian sisters combined. Jackie had traded her thin wire frames for an obnoxious pair of red cat-eye glasses that matched her lipstick and swimsuit.

"Were you even invited here?" Jackie said with a hand gripping her hip.

Her short bob haircut had been straightened so much that it looked like a synthetic wig.

"Yes, Blaine invited me."

Stephanie glared at me from head to toe. Jackie smiled sarcastically.

"Where's your blue-haired friend? Thought you'd be hanging with her tonight instead of coming here, trying to hook up with Blaine," Jackie said.

"Your apology meant nothing?" I asked.

Stephanie stepped in closer. "My apology meant nothing. Blaine was playing games with us and forced us to send those, so yeah, I'm not sorry." She took another step toward me and leaned into my face. "Since you're here, let me tell you exactly how we feel—"

"You two can leave now," Blaine said, handing me a can of Dr Pepper.

Jackie's mouth gaped open, and eyes widened. "Excuse me? Blaine, I thought you didn't invite her so we can work on getting back together. Then this piece of trash shows up, and I'm asked to leave? Are you serious right now?"

I popped open the soda can and sprayed a fine mist of condensation on Jackie. I smiled.

Blaine raised his chin, pinching his lips into a white slash. "Get out of here, Jackie. It's over. You're delusional. We're never getting back together. You were only invited because I felt sorry for you. You're pathetic."

Jackie gave Blaine an intense stare. "I'll call the cops."

"If you do that, you'll regret it." Blaine's voice turned grim with a threatening undertone.

Jackie smirked at me. "Hey, precious, did you know Blaine sells Lapse? One phone call and he's in the pokey—and you've got no boyfriend."

Stephanie doubled over in laughter as Blaine wrapped his hand around Jackie's arm and pulled her up the steps toward the house. I felt a little light-headed, not sure what to believe. If this was true, I knew how my dad would feel about me staying at this party.

"You should know what Blaine's saying about you, sweetheart," Stephanie said.

"And what's that?" I avoided eye contact with

her as I scanned the pool area.

"Ha! I'm sure you can figure that out, given your history."

I glared at her. "What the hell are you talking about? We have no history."

"There's a reason why all the guys are flirting with you. They all think they have a chance. Maybe you shouldn't send such strong signals if you don't want to be known as Easy-Breezy Murphy." She cackled like an old hag. "Yeah, that's what your new boyfriend so lovingly called you. Don't believe me, just ask around."

"That is not true." My lip may have quivered.

"Ah, did I hurt your easy-breezy feelings?"

Pandemonium erupted inside the house, and everyone from the pool area rushed toward the chaos. I bit my lip and followed the herd.

"That crazy witch spritzed me with voodoo juice when I opened the door. She was chanting some devil crap. What the hell is her problem?" Blaine shouted and marched around the living room. There were clusters of red, green, and white balloons — each topped with a sombrero balloon.

"Blaine, calm down. It's just the old lady down the street. We all know she's insane," a guy from my health class said.

I snapped a photo of Blaine's outburst and spotted a single red balloon hovering in front of one of the arrangements. Unlike the others, it wasn't tied down with a ribbon. Nobody seemed to notice anything peculiar as it moved across the room toward me, so I pushed "Record" to make a video of the thing. Blaine's frenzy had commanded everyone's attention, and phones were in the air recording the scene.

Don, Blaine's stepbrother with the frizzy cloud of blond hair and black-rimmed glasses, walked down the staircase. The cast around his wrist was gone, and he wore an Ace bandage in its place.

"Nope, do not come downstairs," Blaine screamed, pointing at the stairs. "Get back to your room, nerd, or you'll be sorry you ever crawled out of your mama."

The balloon crept in my direction, but the attention in the room had diverted to Don. I ended the video, switched to the camera, and took a few more photos of it hanging in the air among the chaos.

"Blaine, you're such a jerk. Nobody can stand you, ya know," Stephanie said. She stormed up the stairs and took Don by the hand. They disappeared into the upstairs hallway.

A group of girls standing behind me babbled about how Stephanie and Don had recently started dating, but that she had tried to keep it all a secret. In my opinion, they didn't look like they belonged together. I stood alone in the living room by the back door, waiting for Blaine to finish ranting to his friends about how much he couldn't stand his stepbrother. I spotted Jackie perched on the armrest of a white leather couch, her eyes puffy from crying. She flashed me an obscene gesture, and I took a picture of it, laughing to myself.

Just as the red balloon curved around the sofa to make its final route toward me, bushy-haired Lynda approached with a bright smile on her face. It was no surprise she was wearing a swimsuit the color of a highlighter.

"I don't know what to say about my friends. They're usually really nice."

I laughed. "Really? I can't imagine that."

Lynda smiled. "You have every right to say that." She shook her head. "But I'm glad you came. It's good to get out and meet people when you're new in town. We're not all bad."

I pressed my lips into a straight line, not knowing how to respond, as I didn't want to say anything that could be used against me or offend the one friendly face in the room.

"Can I ask you something?" she asked.

"Sure." I took a long, soothing drink of Dr Pepper.

"Why isn't Andrea here? I mean, I'm just asking since you two seemed to have become fast friends."

I cocked my head to the side to ponder her question. I had figured she would know about everyone's history. Why would I be the one to ask?

"Um, Blaine didn't invite her—that's all I know."

"You know they're a couple, right? After Blaine broke up with Jackie, they hooked up but hid it— just like Stephanie and Don. I have a knack for finding out stuff. Since you'd become friends with her, I figured you knew."

It took few seconds to process, and then it hit me. "Blaine and Andrea?" I recalled Andrea had said she and her boyfriend hadn't gone public yet. But they didn't seem attracted to each other when he drove us home, and they certainly didn't look like they fit together as a couple.

"Chatting about how handsome I am, huh," Blaine said with a coy smile as he approached.

Lynda tilted her head to the side. "You know it, cuz," she said with a smirk. "This piece of work's my cousin, you know." She rolled her eyes and stepped away, merging with the Stephanie-and-Don-gossip group.

"Can I ask you something in private?" I asked.

"Say no more," he said, taking me by the hand. He guided me up the staircase, and a few others cheered as he unbuttoned his shirt. I rolled my eyes and shook my head—they believed something besides a private conversation was going to happen between Blaine and me.

He pulled me down the hall and opened the first door on the right. As soon as my feet hit the white plush carpet of his bedroom, he stopped and plucked something from his pocket. He set it on his desk. It was a switchblade knife with an ivory handle. We made our way across the room, and he directed me onto the bed. After he pressed a button on a remote he retrieved from the nightstand, a slow, romantic song faded in as flames flickered to life within a rectangular fireplace in the wall. He pressed another button and the drapes closed.

"Blaine, this is not what I meant. I just wanted to talk about some things I heard out there."

He removed his shirt, tossed it on the floor, and smiled. My instinct told me I shouldn't have allowed myself to be alone with him in his room.

"Why are you taking that off?" I asked, sitting up.

"Duh, that old loon sprayed voodoo juice on me. Chill." He rolled his eyes. I stood up, and he pushed my shoulders, urging me to sit back down. "Okay, we can talk first — what's on your mind?" His charismatic demeanor turned scornful. He broke eye contact and stared into the fire as he turned down the music volume and dropped into his desk chair.

"Jackie said you sell drugs. Is this true?"

Blaine laughed and shook his head. "You believe that psychopath? She's my ex and knows I'm attracted to you. C'mon, Shana. I know you're smarter than that."

I studied his face, and he gazed into my eyes without looking away. "Stephanie said you've spread rumors about me and gave me a mean nickname."

He chuckled. "Easy-Breezy Murphy?"

Heat flushed through my body. "Yes. Why would you do that?" I clenched my teeth, wanting to punch the wall.

"I maybe said that. Locker-room talk. Who cares? It's not like you gotta salvage a reputation at school. You don't know these people; we're all about to graduate and part ways. You can stomach a few bad looks in the halls for a few weeks, so just grow some thick skin."

I had to get out of there. My vision clouded, and the room started to spin. Furious at myself for not realizing his motives sooner, I jumped to my feet. The doorbell rang. He stepped in front of me.

"You need to answer the door, and I'm out of here."

He grabbed for my hands, but I yanked them away. I tried to step around him, but he blocked my path.

"There are plenty of people who can get the door. So, are we done with the inquisition?" He clutched my shoulders. "Let's drop the nonsense and get back to what we came here for."

I pulled away from his grip. "I'm going home." I stormed out of the room. As I stepped into the hallway and shut his door, he shouted a string of obscenities and threw something against the wall.

I bounded down the staircase just as the front door swung open. It was Andrea.

"Having a party without me, guys?"

11-RIPPER HOUSE

"Shana?" Andrea said with her eyes bulging. I stopped in my tracks on the bottom stair, and she hurried over to face me. "So, this is why you couldn't come over tonight?" Blaine descended the stairs behind me, buttoning the cuffs of a new shirt. She glared at him and then cut sharp eyes back to me. "You're with him?"

Jackie shrieked as she rushed toward us. "Blaine, are you serious right now? You took this tramp to your room?"

A crowd formed, with phones rising to record the scene.

"Jackie, I'm not a tramp, and he doesn't want you anymore, so get over it." I took in a few calming breaths. "Andrea, it's not what you think."

Too many people had encircled us for me to make a clean break for the door.

"Oh, sure. It looks like you two were just up in his bedroom having a conversation about how much he loves me, right? That's why he was putting his clothes back on?"

With clenched fists, I shook my head. Blaine brushed by me, moved through the group, and made his way toward the back door, shoving Jackie out of the way. It was apparent that he wasn't interested in defending me.

"Andrea, I had no idea. You said you hadn't gone public, for whatever reason, with your new boyfriend. You never mentioned his name, so am I supposed to be psychic?"

Jackie let out a bloodcurdling scream and marched toward us. "Are you serious, Andrea? Blaine broke up with me for you? A creepy Goth girl with choppy Smurf hair? Gross. Well, I'm glad he's cheating on you, so you can see what it feels like."

Andrea glared at Jackie. "Yes, Jackie, he loves me. He wanted to wait until after graduation to announce our relationship because he thinks you're an unstable psychopath and feared for my well-being."

This was more drama than I'd ever witnessed before in my life, and my dad had always been part of the Boston underworld. I made a move to force my way through the group.

"I'm leaving. It was a mistake coming here. I wasn't with him and have zero plans to ever be with him. By the way, he's a serious loser, so enjoy yourself."

Heckles, jeers, and laughter ensued. Nobody would move out of my way. Taunts and exaggerations about Blaine and me flew from all directions. I would never have come to the party had I known that this guy was with Andrea, or that he was a drug dealer, or that he was a misogynistic pig.

Andrea grabbed me by the arm. Twisting to release myself from her grip, I felt something cold as ice connect with my back. Instinctively I spun around and faced the red balloon, hovering behind me. Without thinking, I swatted at it but struck Andrea in the face by accident.

"I thought we were friends, but now that I see your true colors, I'll tell you all about the house you're living in, Shana," Andrea said, checking to see if her nose had bloodied.

"Ripper House," someone shouted from the mass.

"Yeah, everyone knows, Shana. You live in Ripper House. Everyone who's ever lived there has gone psycho and killed people. Sweet little Merry Biggs went home that day, took her dad's gun, and shot up her mother's party before jumping out the attic window to her death. Get out of here. Go home to the house of psychos."

The room faded into the distance, and I struggled to remain conscious as a sudden chill struck my core.

Then I took a page from my father's book of rage. "You have no idea who you're messing with, Andrea. Right next door to you, in Ripper House, lives one of the most dangerous men on the planet. My father and his friends won't be happy to hear how you, and everyone else in here, have treated me."

Another outburst of laughter arose.

"Shana, come here," Don shouted from the top of the staircase.

The balloon lingered as if it had joined the cynics and intimidators. With the conflict escalating, I quickly weighed my options and ran up the stairs, following Don into his bedroom, which was one door down from Blaine's room.

Stephanie was pulling the drapes open as we entered the room. Like the rest of the home, it had a modern flair with a half-cork-strip wall and two light fixtures hanging from the ceiling inside large balls of twine. A glass desk was flush against the windowsill with two laptops, a PC, and a few mobile devices scattered among an array of notepads and writing utensils.

"Shana, please sit down." Stephanie ushered me to the bed and waited for me to get settled. "Don and I have talked this whole situation through, and I apologize. This time, it comes from the heart."

I sighed. She had already retracted one apology, and I was skeptical, so I remained quiet.

"Jackie's my best friend, and I've let her poison my mind. I've been following her lead like a sheep. I'm not a mean person—" She came to a stop and swallowed. I may have had a foul look of disbelief on my face. "To show you I'm serious, I'll stand up to her and tell her this isn't okay. You've been treated horribly since you got here, and that's not right."

She sat down beside me and gazed into my eyes before bowing her head in remorse. Don grinned and nodded in support of her as he took a seat in his desk chair.

"Wow, Stephanie. This is unexpected. Right after I made an entire room hate me, you pull a twist like this."

"Nobody hates you, Shana. Nobody even knows you. We heard everything, and everyone's being stupid. People feed on drama. I'll do what I can to defuse the situation."

"I will, too, not that many people listen to me," Don added.

I sorted my thoughts. "I don't know what he said to everyone about me, but — "

"No worries," she interrupted. "Guys lie. We all know that. No offense, Don."

"None taken. You know I'm not like that," he said.

"But what did Blaine say about me? I don't even know him! Why'd he give me that horrible nickname?"

Stephanie and Don exchanged glances. Don bowed his head. "He's a narcissistic jerk and only cares about one thing—Blaine Walker. He spread a rumor to all his buddies that you and he maybe did some stuff on the plane," he said.

"Did some stuff?"

"You know, that you two went to the restroom and hooked up," Stephanie said.

They gauged my reaction to see if the rumor was true. It couldn't have been further from the truth. My mouth fell open, and I groaned, clenching my fists.

"He is a bold-faced liar. The furthest we got is exchanging names. How could he do this to me? He's a monster! Don, you were on the plane. Did you see us go to the bathroom together?"

"See, I've been asked that before, and all I can say is I didn't see either of you use the lavatory. However, I wasn't looking the whole time. I was working on a take-home calculus exam. But I'd believe you over Blaine any day. I hate that guy."

Stephanie rubbed my shoulder. "This is exactly why we all need to get revenge on the sick jerk."

"Revenge?" I looked out the window. The fog had nearly dissipated, and I could see my house at the top of the hill on the other side of Tabatha's shanty cottage. My eyes cut to his desk, and I spotted a pair of binoculars. I bolted toward the window for a better view. There was a perfect line of sight to my bedroom window. Next to the binoculars was a Post-it Note with my phone number written on it. My thoughts scrambled to understand.

"You." I turned to face Don. "You've been texting me the photos. You're the one!" I sprinted to the bedroom door.

"No, wait. I..." Don's voice faded away as I slammed his door shut, hurried down the hall, and entered the first room I could find.

The emotional breakdown I'd been fighting emerged, and I threw myself on the bed, sobbing until I got the courage to walk through the crowd of adversaries downstairs and go home to Ripper House. I stood up, heavy-eyed with a pounding headache, and prepared myself to endure the name-calling on my journey to the front door. I crept into the hall. Upstairs was quiet, all doors were closed, but laughter and loud voices rumbled from below. The open space underneath the closed door across from Don's room caught my attention. There was a dark substance oozing onto the light wood flooring. I bent down and raked a finger through it. The thick liquid was warmer than room temperature, and it turned a scarlet hue on my fingertip. The hint of metallic copper brought me back to Hugo as he struggled for his final breaths. It was blood.

12-A PERSON OF INTEREST

Instinct drove me to turn the door handle, and when I pushed the door, it hit something. I could see that it was a bathroom. Pressing my body against the door for strength, I shoved it open enough for me to walk through. I stood motionless, staring at the body on the floor. Caramel hair, bloodstained peach shirt, navy shorts. It was Blaine. I scrambled to comprehend what could have happened. I reached out for his shoulder and rolled him over to his back. His eyes stared at the ceiling as if he had seen a ghost, and a knife with an ivory handle protruded from his chest. I panicked, yanked it out of the wound, and tossed it across the bathroom.

"Blaine!"

I slapped his face, but he didn't respond. I leaned toward his mouth, but no breaths hit my cheek. I pressed two fingers against his wrist, but there was no pulse. I screamed until my throat gave out, and slowly a crowd formed. As I scrambled to my feet, I realized I was covered in his blood. Accusations flew, and Jackie let out a deafening scream. Three people held her back from attacking me.

"I didn't do it! I found him like this!"

Don emerged from the mass. "I've called the police, and my parents are coming home now. Everybody downstairs. Nobody leave—this is a crime scene."

While a portion of the hysterical group stayed in the hallway at the bathroom's entrance to scream at me, part of the mob took to the staircase and assembled in the living room. I could hear the kids below arguing. I walked over to the sink and rinsed the blood from my hands as the kids in the hall shouted, calling me a murderer. The red balloon loomed in the hall, floating behind a boy in my physiology class, and I inhaled a slow breath. The guy took a few steps into the bathroom and approached me at the sink.

"Why'd you kill him, Shana? Because he told everyone what you guys did on the plane?" he asked as a tear streamed down his cheek.

"I said I didn't do it. One of you did, though, so you need to be careful and figure out who the murderer is." I dried my hands with a hand towel. When I turned back to give him a dirty look, the hallway was empty.

The last one to walk down the stairs, I texted my parents with 911, which was our family's unoriginal code for an emergency. I scrolled up to read a message from my mother from a couple of hours before about her being concerned my father was engaged in a plot to murder Vincent Byrne and take the reins back in Boston. It wasn't like her to put that level of sensitive information in writing, so I realized she was losing her mind. I was sad I hadn't responded, but she replied she'd be over at Blaine's house in minutes. The group downstairs had divided into criers and consolers, and it sounded like a teenage day care. Eyes burned into me as I stood against the wall by the back door to wait for the police. With a face swollen from crying, Jackie gave me a sarcastic grin, and then stood up in front of the group.

"Let's kill some time until the cops get here." She wiped her cheeks. "Why don't we discuss Ripper House? Does anyone know the history? I do!"

As she garnered the crowd's attention, the hysteria seemed to calm.

Jackie sneered in my direction before she began her lecture. "Back in the twenties, there was a famous serial killer called the Butcher of Noxhelm. He appropriated an old cemetery and built Ripper House on the land, claiming he wanted to draw upon the power of the dead to give him superhuman strength to complete his life's mission. Legend has it that he killed more than eighty young girls. Some were even buried on the property in the crawl spaces."

Gasps and moans rang out. I turned toward the back window and peered out at the pool area.

Stephanie walked over and stood beside me. Don followed.

"Jackie, do you know the story of what happened with Merry Biggs?" the guy from my physiology class asked.

"Why, yes, I do."

Stephanie moaned, exchanging looks of irritation with Don. "I'm sorry about this, but there's nothing I can do right now without making a spectacle," she whispered in my ear. Jackie caught sight of her beside me and paused with a scowl.

"Why aren't the police here yet?" A girl with a pointed nose and pixie haircut burst into tears. "She needs to be arrested! We can't sit here and have story time while she gets to just stand there, free."

People rushed over to comfort her, rubbing her back and promising the police were on their way.

Jackie glared at me. She cleared her throat to ensure she had everyone's attention. "Merry Biggs's mother sold jewelry and hosted parties where her friends would come over for tea and peruse her collection. The day of the massacre, she was hosting what she had called on the invitation a Red Party. She had launched a line of ruby jewelry, so she decorated the house in red, served red food, and asked everyone to wear red hats. Merry had been visiting her friend down the street and came home while the bash was going on. Something incensed her, and she grabbed her dad's gun from the closet and went on a shooting spree. Some say she had taken drugs that made her crazy." She paused to absorb her audience's reaction. "Then, someone posted the gruesome crime scene online with the caption 'The Devil's Party.' It was a grisly sight, with red balloons and streamers among blood-splattered walls and bodies lying about in Noxhelm County Morgue bags."

Another round of gasps followed as sirens blasted outside. Police officers charged through the front door. My parents were behind them, and they dashed across the room toward me. Another round of hysteria arose in the room, and the kids rushed to give the police their versions of what had happened.

"Are you all right, Shana?" my mother asked as she examined me from head to toe.

"What happened?" my father asked with pinched brows.

My lip began to quiver. "A boy was stabbed, upstairs in a bathroom. This isn't my blood; it's his. Don't be surprised if everyone here blames me, but you know I would never do—"

"Of course not, that's ludicrous," my mother said with fury in her eyes.

After explaining how I had discovered the body and pulled out the knife, my dad grabbed his phone.

"Wait, you can't call Richard," my mother said.

"Give me a break. I can't call anyone else. Richard's always been there for me—there's nobody better. He's an attorney. It's not like he's gonna call Vince and give us up."

"He's in Massachusetts. Don't you need a state license to practice law?"

"He has firms on both coasts, dear. His West Coast office is in San Fran. He's licensed in Cali."

He put in a call to Richard Nugent, who agreed to jump on the next flight.

At least an hour passed. We were instructed not to speak to one another and not to move. The forensic techs buzzed about collecting evidence, and the detectives took each one of us in separate rooms for interviews. We were all processed with fingerprints, photographed from every angle, and made to give a blood sample. They also ran a forensic vacuum over our bodies.

A dark-complected investigator in a tan business suit and military haircut approached me. "I'm Detective Damian Shockley, a homicide investigator from the Noxhelm PD. I'd like to ask you a few questions. May we step outside?"

I waited for my parents' lead.

My father answered. "I'm Ian Murphy, and this is my wife, Bronnie-Jo. This is our daughter, Shana, and we live a couple of houses down. Just moved here from Bost—" He cleared his throat. "Chicago."

Detective Shockley skewed his head to the side and narrowed his eyes with a trace of suspicion in his expression.

"We don't mind stepping outside so you can ask Shana some questions, but we'd prefer to be present," my mother said as she took my hand.

My parents had made a game-time decision not to make a stand about an attorney being present for questioning, to avoid raising suspicions. Nobody else in the room had an attorney, but their parents were arriving in droves.

"There goes the most dangerous man in the world. Be careful, guys—you don't want to mess with that family," a male voice jeered as my dad opened the door. "Hey, Officer, stay vigilant!"

My father cast a wrathful glance at me, knowing I had opened my big mouth. We gathered onto the front porch, and the detective shut the door.

"I'm not going to sugarcoat this. You're shaping up to be the prime suspect. Your fingerprints are on the knife—"

"I pulled it out by mistake. I'm sorry—I panicked."

My mother tugged on my arm. "Shana, let him speak."

"Young lady, you are covered in the victim's blood. You were seen with the body when it was discovered. Nearly everyone in here says you did it." He crossed his arms over his chest and stared directly into my eyes.

"I just moved here, and everyone in there hates me. I didn't even really know the guy and was trying to leave this party."

"You were trying to leave, and they wouldn't allow it?"

"They blocked my path. And then I went up to Don's room, where I found binoculars that were pointed toward my bedroom."

The detective nodded. "We heard that story.

Those binoculars didn't belong to Don. They were taken from Blaine's room earlier today, which strengthens your motive against Blaine. So the victim was stalking you?"

"All right, that's enough. My daughter will not answer another question without an attorney present. Unless you're charging her with a crime, we'll be going home now."

Detective Shockley grinned and rubbed his chin. "We need to process the trace analysis before any charges are filed. That might save you or put a lock on this case. Go home. I know where you live." He peered over his shoulder toward our house and raised a single eyebrow as if to suggest he knew all about Ripper House.

13-MOLES

My mother was about to make breakfast the next morning when Damian Shockley knocked on our door just after nine. My father answered, and I eavesdropped from the entryway to the dining room.

"May I come in? I would like to speak to your daughter. There are some follow-up questions we need answered before we can move forward with this case."

My dad rubbed the back of his neck, and his face flushed a bright crimson. "I've already told you, unless you are charging her with a crime; we have no business with you. My daughter will not answer any questions unless our attorney is present. He will be here by noon today."

Without allowing the detective to respond, he clicked the door shut and then grabbed a painting from the wall and threw it across the room. My mother scurried from the kitchen to see what was going on.

"We're screwed. It's over. They'll be here any minute. This time he'll be smart and take out the whole family—not just me. I'll probably have to watch them kill you both first." He stormed around the room searching for more things to throw.

"As we discussed last night, don't be foolish, Ian—"

"Cullen." His hands clenched and unclenched, and then he punched a wall. "Call me Cullen. I'm not playing this silly witness protection game any longer. It's done. I'm Cullen O'Sullivan from Boston. I'm not hiding like a rat anymore."

"Does that mean I can call Monica and log in to my Yipper accounts now?"

My parents simultaneously shouted, "No!"

My mom stomped back into the kitchen, and we both followed. "Dad, I never said we were from Boston—they don't know our real names! Don't do this."

He slammed a fist on the table. "There are moles in every police department. When we entered the program, they took your prints and put you into the system. You were printed last night at that boy's house. By now they've found out about your identity and know who we are. The feds put us in their system when we became part of this stupid program in case any of our bodies turned up in a ditch somewhere."

My mother advanced toward him and spoke in a peaceful tone. "Cullen, if you would have followed their rules from the start, we'd still be safe. First, I'm sure when they tag her prints, it won't give our address — it probably just flags something, like tells them to contact the US Marshals. If there are moles, the marshals know that, too. I'm more worried about what you've been doing with the boys in Boston to let Vince know where we are — far more than Shana getting printed in this small town. Plus, they only referenced the prints at the scene, they probably didn't even run them in the Automated Fingerprint Identification System — they're all local kids."

"Well, Bronnie-Jo, Mickey just let me know Vince boarded a plane to California a few minutes ago with his bimbo, Candy. How do you think he figured out where we were? We're done. And, yes, they always run prints in AFIS. Always."

"Even if there's a mole in the police department, that doesn't mean they have access to our address. Like I said, it probably just has a flag or something to notify the marshals. We should just lay low and not leave the house."

"How do you know Vince is coming for us? He travels a lot, and California is Aunt Candy's favorite place to go," I said.

My mother nodded. "Shana has a valid point there. If Mickey's still alive, Vince isn't onto you. It's too fast of a turnaround for Shana to be fingerprinted around two in the morning and for Vince to get the news and hop on a plane that quickly. And wouldn't Vince send one of the boys? Why would he come down himself? Why would he bring Candy? It doesn't add up."

My dad grabbed a chair and sat down, his arms folded. "Mickey sent an associate to bring me supplies. He'll be here soon."

"Supplies?" my mother asked.

She poured three mugs of coffee and then grabbed ingredients from the refrigerator for breakfast.

"Guns. We can't protect ourselves. We're sitting ducks."

She threw her arms in the air. "Great, you are letting a Trojan Horse in our home. Have you gone mad as a box of frogs? I hope you trust Mickey with all our lives, because our hearts are literally beating in his hands, and all he has to do is squeeze."

She cracked eggs into a mixing bowl while grinding her teeth. He stood up and grabbed his coffee mug from the counter.

I decided to create a diversion. "While we are on the subject of security, that old lady, mom's new coffee buddy, was in our house yesterday, up in the attic while you guys weren't here."

My mother feigned a smile. "She mentioned wanting to speak to a ghost up there." She sighed. "I humored the crazy old bat. Said she could come over anytime to chat with the, uh, the phantom spirit. I gave her the extra key."

I grabbed my coffee mug, dumped sugar in it, and stirred. "Are you serious, Mother? You gave her a key to our home and said she could come over anytime without us here and have séances upstairs in Creepyville? Have you gone mad as a box of frogs?"

"Shana, she's old. She's delusional and quite harmless. There's nothing here to steal. We have nothing in this place that we care about."

"She stole my candy! Hid it up in the attic until it melted!"

"Oh, the poor thing doesn't have long left on this earth. Let her have your candy." She poured batter into the frying pan.

"Mom, she said she couldn't eat sugar! Or was she lying because she didn't want to eat one of her poison brownies?"

My dad smirked. "I can see Shana's point about the candy. I'd be mad, too. I mean, it's candy. Candy shouldn't be wasted like that."

"Oh, stop it, Cullen." My mom suppressed a giggle. "Shana, the brownies were delicious and a sweet gesture. And if the poor dear believes she's speaking to a ghost who communicates with her dead daughter—so be it. Let the old woman be happy. Sorry, I should have warned you I told her to come by anytime." My mom spun around from the stove to catch my eye. "Sweetheart, you don't believe in ghosts, do you?"

I sighed and drank my coffee slowly. "Obviously, not. All right, fine. If you want to let thieving voodoo witches in our house while we're not here, that's your problem. But look at this." I marched over and handed her my phone, open to the text thread of photos that had been sent to me from the unknown number.

She frowned as she scrolled through them, maximizing each photo to get the fine details. "I don't remember you showing these to the police yesterday?" As if on cue, another message appeared. It was a photo of an article in the Boston Herald about my father and his former colleagues. The headline was from a few years back during a spell of legal trouble: CULLEN O'SULLIVAN—PRIME SUSPECT IN A FEDERAL RACKETEERING SCANDAL.

"Cullen, you've got to see this." She handed the phone to my dad.

My father's eyes narrowed as he pressed his lips into a white line. He scrolled through each photo carefully. My mother tensed, waiting for his reaction.

"Our time's up. I'll handle this and get our lives back."

"What do you mean by that, Cullen?"

"I mean you don't have to worry about anything. I should have handled this from the start. This whole program thing was a mistake."

14–TOXICOLOGY TALES

The following morning, I awoke to the sound of my mother screaming my father's name. Within seconds, my bedroom door clanked against the wall, and she marched inside.

"He's not here. He isn't anywhere! He left us! No note, nothing. He took all of his stuff." Trembling, she paced back and forth across my room.

"Calm down, Mother. He had a reason. He would never abandon us. He knows that someone in town knows who we are. He said he's handling it and for us not to worry. Let's go make breakfast."

We scurried into the kitchen. Like two robots at a factory, she cracked eggs in the frying pan, and I started the coffee. Working in silence to get everything moving, our minds raced through all the possible scenarios of why my father had left. I couldn't come up with a good enough reason for discussion, so I adjusted the focus.

"Mother, I'm well aware you don't believe in ghosts, or anything supernatural, but I need to discuss something else before we talk about Dad."

She gazed at me over her shoulder as she scratched at her cheek. "Go ahead." She lowered the burner flame and twisted around to face me.

"Since we moved to this hellhole, you and Dad have argued nonstop and left me to fight with this house."

"Fight with this house?" She turned to flip the eggs and then glanced around the room as if searching for answers.

"This house isn't right. The kids at school call this place Ripper House, and everyone who's ever lived here goes nuts. A serial killer built it over a cemetery."

She threw her head back and laughed, turning up the flames on the burner. I grabbed two mugs and poured the coffee.

"C'mon, Shana. Kids are famous for creating urban legends. These are small-town minds, bored with their lives, so they make up something interesting to talk about. Don't take a ride on their boloney train. I thought you were smarter than that!"

I tossed three sugar cubes into my coffee and a Splenda packet into my mother's mug.

"Ugh, Well, this freaking weird balloon—"

"Stop with the balloon story, or I'll get you a shrink." She waved her spatula at me.

"I'm not joking, Mother. At Blaine's house, the

thing followed me around, and when it touched me, it felt like an ice cube. Is helium cold?"

She squinted her eyes. "I suppose when the gas comes out of the tank, it may be a little cool."

I stirred the coffee in the mugs and walked over to put her cup beside her. "No, the latex demon was as cold as a freezer when it brushed against me."

"Shana, you went to a party decorated with balloons. Maybe one got sucked up next to a cold vent for a while? Please never mention this again, or people will think you're crazy—and we cannot afford that right now."

She pulled four slices of bacon from the package, arranged them on a paper plate, and slid them in the microwave.

"Ugh. If I could call Monica, she'd understand. Can I please call her? Dad said we're not under the program anymore. They know who we are, so who cares? She'd never tell anyone where we are!"

She shook her head back and forth and guided the eggs onto the plates. "For your own good, no. Sorry I didn't discuss this with you when we got back last night, but Dad and I spoke with Mr. Nugent at the Noxhelm Bed & Breakfast. He's staying all week to deal with the police for you. He's instructed us to resume our normal routines, but we are not to speak with anyone about the case. He doesn't want you leaving the house until Monday for school. Therefore, no, we're still not allowed to contact anybody in Boston. As things stand, only Mickey and Mr. Nugent know where we are—and we're supposed to trust them."

"Mom, our cover is so blown. Dad is who knows where, Mickey was sending someone here with guns, some creep in town knows who we are, and Vince is on his way to California—and might even end up on our doorstep. I think a call to my best friend won't hurt."

"Yes, it could, Shana. But I need to talk to Mr. Nugent about your dad leaving. I wonder if he knows why he left." She dropped the bread in the toaster. I took a big sip of my coffee and turned on the tiny television.

"Isn't he going to take care of Vince? Isn't Vince the reason we're here?"

"Shana, Vince is on his way to California. If Dad wanted to face Vince, he wouldn't have left." She grabbed a knife to butter the toast. "Turn the channel to the news."

I sighed. "Okay."

The doorbell rang. We froze, gazing into each other's widened eyes. I lunged over to turn off the TV, and she swatted my hand away and shook her head no. We tiptoed through the living room and did our best to peer out the drapes to see the porch. Tabatha Gill stood there. Ignoring my protests, my mother exhaled as she swung open the door.

"Good morning, dear. Come in. Are you hungry? I just made breakfast."

Tabatha's beady eyes turned into slits as she stared at me. "Certainly, I would love that."

I wasn't happy with my mom for inviting her inside. We moved to the kitchen, and my mother poured her a cup of coffee. Then, I remembered her stopping by Blaine's party.

"Ms. Gill." I grabbed my coffee, took the seat beside her, and spoke loudly enough for my mother to catch every word. "Blaine Walker, the boy who was murdered Friday night, said you chanted words at him and spritzed him with a liquid. Why did you do that?"

I had forgotten about the incident and became angry at myself for not telling the police. I hoped one of the other kids that had been interviewed had reported what she had done.

Tabatha sneered at me as she accepted her coffee from my mother. She took a long swig. My mom hadn't seen her reaction to me, but became interested in what she had to say and walked over to take a seat at the table.

"I offered the power of sight to the young man. He needed the sight to live. But those with a darkened soul are incapable of benefiting from the spell, so that is why he met his fate."

"Mother! Do you hear this?"

She arose from the table and used tongs to remove the bacon from the plate. We sat in silence as she finished preparing breakfast. It was a good thing that my mother always made extra food when she cooked.

"Ms. Gill, are you saying you knew the boy was going to be killed?" She delivered the plates to the table.

"Why, yes. I knew he was doomed unless he could see his destiny. I was unable to save the boy. Very unfortunate."

She took a bite of her eggs and ran a slice of bacon in the runny yolk. I heard the word Boston on the television and swiveled around to watch the news report.

"Mom, look." I pointed to the TV.

She turned up the volume as we watched the report of a teenager at my old school in Boston who had shot and murdered four friends while under the influence of the drug Lapse.

"Oh no. Do you know that girl?" my mom asked.

A photograph flashed on the screen. The girl had been in my art class, but she wasn't in my circle. I cringed as they listed the four victims. I knew them all, and I was relieved they weren't close to me. One of the deceased was the girl who'd come up with my nickname Clown Wig.

The doorbell rang. My mother asked Tabatha to remain at the table, and we glided into the living room to the window.

"The one at the door isn't a foe, dear," Tabatha said.

My mom caught sight of her. "It's Andrea from next door."

My emotions split in two. I was relieved the visitor wasn't a mobster but annoyed by the conflict I had endured with her on Friday night. I figured she was there to accuse me of being a murderer.

"I'll get it." I grabbed the handle of the front door. "This may not go well, but I'm all right."

I pulled the door open and invited her inside.

"First of all, I just want to say I am truly sorry for how I behaved toward you. I was out of line," she said.

This was unexpected. She fluttered around the foyer as if she had pent-up energy.

"Okay, well, what caused the change of heart?"

"Um, can we go to your room and talk? I have a ton of things to say."

I excused myself to go to the kitchen. "Mom, we'll pick up where we left off later, okay?"

"That's fine. I made an appointment with Mr. Nugent for this afternoon, as well. Take your breakfast with you."

I slapped an egg in between two pieces of toast and made a mobile sandwich. Andrea and I scampered upstairs to my bedroom.

"That creepy woman is at your house again?" she asked as she sank into my plush velvet chair.

"Ugh, I know. My mom's her new BFF."

Andrea grinned, and then her face grew solemn. "I know you didn't kill Blaine, Shana."

"Duh! Of course I didn't!" I rolled my eyes and jumped on my bed. I took a huge bite of my sandwich.

"I'm not even upset he's dead. It's weird, but with everything that happened, I haven't even shed a tear. Am I twisted?" She ran her finger along the seam of the chair, her eyes wide as they awaited my response.

"Blaine was a dreadful person. He hurt a lot of people with no remorse. You're not twisted."

She slapped her hands on her knees and sat upright. "I've been thinking about who did it, and I have it down to three suspects. Did you hear about the autopsy report?"

"No, I've been trying not to think about it, Kind of suffering from a bit of trauma after finding a dead body and finding out I live in Ripper House. Excuse me if I'm not quite myself."

"Sorry about that. I should have kept my mouth shut." She bowed her head for a minute.

I gazed at her for a moment. "Given the circumstances, I get it. So what about the autopsy?" I took another bite, balled up the rest of the sandwich in the paper towel, and tossed it into the trash can by the bed.

"He consumed a large amount of castor oil right before he died." She stood up and walked toward the window. "The timeline of the night suggests you may have been with him when he ingested it—was he drinking or eating anything?" She peered outside and then ambled back to the velvet chair.

"No. What is castor oil and why would he consume it?"

"Um, it's used for constipation. It's a laxative."

"Oh, gosh. He took it at his party?"

"Well, someone may have slipped it into his drink. They're investigating. I was curious if you saw him take anything."

"No, I didn't. So, who do you think murdered him?"

She raised an index finger and arched an eyebrow. "Jackie Morgan. An angry ex, she was on the warpath against you, me, and Blaine. Didn't you see how irrational she was that night?"

I considered Jackie for a moment, but then shook my head. "She's too obvious. Did they find her fingerprints on the knife?"

"Yes, but they lifted many. Yours, mine, Stephanie's, Lynda's." She gazed up at the ceiling. "Oh, and Don's — and obviously Blaine's."

"How did that many people handle the weapon?"

"People said Blaine brought the knife downstairs to show it off. Then he put it away in his bedroom."

"Yeah, I remember him pulling it from his pocket and putting it on his desk. But then, you came to the party much later. How were your prints on it?"

"I was at his house the other day. He showed it to me. He said his uncle gave it to him for his birthday last month."

I moaned. "Why did I pull the knife out of his chest? I'm so stupid!"

"Don't worry, Shana. The killer always gets caught in the end."

Recollecting how many times my father had talked about people who were murdered by his outfit, I disagreed with her but left it alone. "Who else is on your list?"

She held up two fingers. "Number two is Don, his stepbrother. They hated each other more than anybody could ever know. It's weird, but now that Blaine's dead, it's like goggles have been removed, and I see his true personality. I had just started dating him. That whole new relationship euphoria thing blinded me. I see now that Blaine was a cruel person. He was so mean to Don. So, if Don did it, I can't say I'd blame him."

"But why would Don do it at a party with witnesses? He's smart, right?"

"That's the reason why I think he may be the killer. He wanted more people around with motives." Her eyes grew more animated, and she sat up straight. "Oh, and once he told me his real dad is on death row. Have you ever heard of the West Coast Slasher?"

I hesitated as I pondered her question. "I think so, about ten years ago, right? I was a kid when all that was going on."

"Yes, and that's his dad."

"But what does that have to do with him?" I went over to open the drapes.

"Genetics. I took a psychology class. There's research out there that behavior can be passed down through generations."

I didn't agree with either of her choices, as they were both too obvious. "Hmm. All right, who is your third?"

"Lynda Green."

"What? She's too nice, definitely not a killer. She was the only friendly one there."

We avoided eye contact for a moment, bowing

our heads in regret of what had happened at the party.

"Lynda's his cousin."

"Right, she told me that. They seemed to get along fine."

"First, Lynda is Jackie's best friend — so she isn't that nice."

"She always was to me, though." I marched back toward the bed.

"Second to that, their great-aunt recently passed away. A multimillionaire from Stanford, California, she had recently amended her will for an even split between the two, but only if they became roommates during their entire freshman year at Stanford University, for she was an alumnus and a generous donor. In my opinion, it's kind of a manipulative way to force a younger generation of her family to continue the legacy."

"That makes no sense. Were Lynda and Blaine even accepted into Stanford?"

"Before she died, the great-aunt had been told they both had, but that they were weighing options on where to go next fall. However, Lynda was the only one who got the acceptance letter. Blaine lied to his parents about it. I found out through Don, who had snooped through his rejection pile. Don told Lynda, and she knew what Blaine had done."

"That's interesting."

We sat in silence for a minute before she continued. "On another note, is it true that your dad is a gangster?"

"Ha! No, he just used to own a gun range back in Chicago. I was mad when I said that about him. He just knows a lot about guns. Just angry words that meant nothing."

My phone vibrated with a text message from an unknown number. My heart sank in my chest. Another photo—me covered in blood on Friday night, standing in the bathroom next to Blaine's body. The caption said, Like father, like daughter. Just confess.

As I did everything possible to suppress a panic attack, the doorbell rang. I couldn't go downstairs because I'd be spotted by whoever stood on the porch. I crept into the hallway, waiting for my mother to give the okay. The front door creaked open, and her voice remained calm, so we walked toward the staircase.

"Shana?" she shouted.

"Yes, Mother?"

"Andrea's parents are here."

Andrea's eyes bulged, and she took the stairs with haste.

"Mom, what's wrong?"

"The police have questions for her. She needs to go down to the station."

15-THE WARNING

With morning sunrays streaming through the slits in the drapes, and my mom channel surfing on the adjacent sofa, I awakened. In one hand she held the remote, and in the other a cup of coffee.

"Have you even slept?" I asked as I rubbed my eyes.

All the color had faded from her face. Her hair was in disarray, and her eye makeup was smudged below her eyes. She shook her head. "I can't, honey. I'm anxious about why your dad left us and if we're safe."

"You haven't heard anything from him?"

"Not a peep. That might be for our safety, though. Or maybe they got to him? I'm so worried."

"Don't be. Dad's an intelligent man, and wouldn't do anything to put us in danger. What I'm more concerned about is that I get a cup of coffee. I see you've made some."

"Yes, of course. I just made a fresh pot. It's my second pot of the day."

Vincent Byrne's photo blasted on the local Noxhelm news report, and she turned up the volume and sat upright.

"Oh, my gosh," I said.

The reporter went on about a story of an infamous crime boss from Boston who had been found dead in his room at the Noxhelm Bed & Breakfast.

"Do you think Dad did this? Isn't that where Mr. Nugent is staying right now?"

She rushed over to the slit in the drapes and peered out the window. I followed her lead. The mist covered anything beyond the street. We could see that there weren't any black SUVs parked right in front of the house at least.

"It's Monday. Should I go to school?"

She grabbed her phone from the coffee table and thumbed through her messages.

"I don't want us to do anything out of the ordinary." She paused and stared at the ceiling. "Mr. Nugent gave strict instructions to proceed with your daily routine. You're a suspect in a murder case. It's best for you to be at school. You need to act normal as far as this court case is concerned. And school's safer than being at home—there are tons of witnesses. Richard's here all week to ensure things get straightened out with you. He's been in contact with Detective Shockley every day." She hesitated. "Yes, he's staying at that same hotel as Vince, but I'm uncertain of what that means. I mean, this town isn't very big. There can't be many choices for lodging."

"Do you think Dad did it?"

"Honestly, no, I don't. Your dad isn't a killer, Shana. But he could have had something to do with his murder indirectly. Don't talk about your case or the Vince situation to anyone while you're at school."

After getting ready, I spent time researching on my own. I perused all the social media accounts belonging to Vincent Byrne to find clues of who murdered him. He hadn't mentioned his travels to California or my aunt Candy in any recent posts, but we knew she had been traveling with him. Her accounts hadn't had a post since the day of my uncle's funeral when she'd posted, "RIP, Cillian O'Sullivan." Since his death had been her fault, her post hadn't sat well with my family.

After browsing a few websites with articles about the West Coast Slasher, I read about how Don's biological dad used to kill his victims by stabbing them in the heart with a knife. I gazed at a grainy picture. He wore dark-rimmed glasses, had blond, frizzy hair to his shoulders, and he had acne riddling his cheeks. He and Don could have been identical twins.

Next I checked my Boston friends' posts, and it saddened me to see they hadn't posted about me since the previous Thursday. A lifetime of friendship, and after a couple of days, they had nothing else to say. Monica had been silent on social media altogether, which was disheartening.

After checking the front steps for Andrea, I scanned the student accounts from Noxhelm High. On Yipper, I paused at a posted video of me and Stephanie arguing in the cafeteria on my first day at school. The comments were split in favor between us, but I stopped reading them to prevent myself from getting angry and responding. Farther down the feed were all about Friday's murder. Many featured me, and some accused others. As I scrolled through the thread of photos and videos taken that night, a post from Blaine Walker emerged on the screen, dated Monday, May 8. Sorry I had to crap out on the party. A POV picture of the bathroom before the murder was included with the post. The post said just now as the time stamp. I took a screenshot as Andrea rang the doorbell. I said goodbye to my mother, and she insisted on a hug before I hurried away and joined Andrea on the porch. Her blue hair had been cut into short bangs and dyed a chestnut brown.

"Wow, I love your hair, it looks great!"

"Thanks. Mom made me do it before my interview with the investigator." She bowed her head as she turned around. "I didn't want to, but she didn't give me a choice."

With a normal hair color, peach nail polish, minimal makeup, and a yellow T-shirt, she made me realize how minor adjustments, when combined, could make you seem like a different person.

"I'm dying to know what all went down yesterday," I said as we skipped down the front steps. "Tell me everything. What did they want with you?"

She shrugged her shoulders with a quick raise of her eyebrows. "Honestly, nothing. They were just following up on the interview from Friday night. I think they're seeing if anyone is changing their story or has new information. They'll probably ask you to come in again, as well."

My sixth sense told me she was hiding something. Futile to press further, I changed the subject to our upcoming English literature test for the rest of the walk to school. When we arrived, I was prepared to combat the comments about me being a killer, but nobody said a word about it to me as I walked down the halls.

The exam in first period wasn't difficult, as I had already studied the novel at my old school. I arrived in physiology in high spirits to find Jackie and Lynda engaged in a heated discussion about Blaine's murder. Jackie was more subdued with her wire frames and a cashmere tank top, and Lynda had ditched the neon garb and opted for a pale-blue top. Don wasn't in his seat. In the trophy hallway by the front office, Don Walker's name was plastered all over the perfect attendance awards.

"Shana, have the police brought you in for questioning yet?" Lynda asked.

Jackie's eyes were red and swollen. As I lowered into my seat, she gave a look of genuine sadness.

"No, I haven't. Have you?"

Lynda responded. "Yes, both of us went in. They

just asked us repeat questions from Friday night. Not sure what any of it helped, but they're concerned with who gave him the castor oil. Did you hear about that?"

"Yes, Andrea mentioned they discovered it during the autopsy."

"I just got to school. I've been at the station since seven a.m. They found the bottle of oil and are testing it to see if it is the same as what he ingested. They recovered the bottle in the trash at Blaine's house," Lynda continued.

Thrilled the police had changed their focus, I hid a grin. The evidence against me was purely circumstantial, and I didn't have anything to do with the castor oil. I was confident this new evidence would vindicate me. Ignoring my mother's warning about talking about the case, I brought up the mysterious post.

"Did you guys see the post from Blaine's account this morning, on Yipper?"

"Someone posted from Blaine's account?" Jackie muttered.

I nodded. "Yep, right before school." Lynda took my phone and viewed the screenshot. They both grabbed their phones to open their Yipper app and scrolled through the feed.

"There's no post. Are you sure the post was from today? It's not there."

"I was scrolling through when it popped up with today's date."

"His parents must have made Yipper take it

down. Who has access to his accounts? Who would do that?" Lynda asked.

"A sicko, that's who," Jackie said.

"I suppose somebody with his password or access to his devices if he saves his log-in information. In other words, it could be anyone. A rather sick joke, though. Seems premeditated, doesn't it? I mean, who would have thought to take a picture of that bathroom where he died?" I asked.

"I'll tell you who—the murderer! The detective gave me his business card. I'm going to text him and let him know about this right now," Jackie said.

"I'm sure he already knows, but it's a good lead," I said.

For the first time, Jackie acted pleasantly toward me. I couldn't believe she didn't accuse me of killing Blaine. It was a 180-degree turn around from how I'd been treated on Friday night. I supposed Stephanie had stayed true to her word and had spoken with her.

At lunch, Lynda and Stephanie sat with Andrea and me. Surreal to all sit together without conflict, it also showed how fragile teenage emotions truly were. Against the trend of conservative appearances, Stephanie had a bright-paisley scarf tied around a messy bun and wore huge yellow hoop earrings that matched her jumpsuit.

"You all know now—Don and I are dating." She threw her palms up. "And, Shana, that's why I didn't like you when you first moved here. Don said he saw you on the plane, and that you were pretty,"

Stephanie blurted as she put her tray on the table. "I've already apologized twice, but once again, I'm sorry for how I treated you."

Lynda puckered her lips and gave a low chuckle of amusement. "I don't get what the attraction is to Nerd Boy, but he's nice — I'll give him that. Where is he today?"

"His parents wanted him to stay at home to help with the funeral arrangements and to clean out Blaine's room. His mother isn't well."

"I can imagine." I lowered my head for a moment. "Oh, Lynda, I heard you got into Stanford. Congratulations, that's quite an accomplishment."

She stiffened her posture and cocked her head to the side, trying to read my expression. "How'd you know about that?"

"Andrea told me. She said you were accepted, and that's where you are going in the fall. You should be very proud."

"Andrea told you about that? Hmm." She stared at her lunch tray in deep thought.

"Was it a secret or something?" I asked.

Lynda shrugged a shoulder. "I suppose not. Thanks."

After school, I found the counselor's office to attend the mandatory session I was assigned because of the incidents on my first day at school.

"Shana, I think you know why you're here, right?" the counselor asked as she flicked her pen against the desk. She reeked of recent college graduate and couldn't have been a day over twenty-two.

"Yes. On my first day here, a couple of girls bullied me. It's all worked out now."

"I see." She took a few minutes to write notes on her yellow legal pad.

"I didn't even say that much for you to write all that down."

"I make notes about everything. Now, how did the move from" — she looked at my file — "Chicago make you feel? Did you feel overwhelmed?"

There was no way for me to explain all I had been through, and I wasn't about to tell her anything that scratched the surface.

"Yes, I felt extremely stressed. I'm much better now, and the girls and I are getting along great. Can I go home now?"

I received a text message and opened it as the counselor read from a pamphlet about stress hormones. Adrenaline blasted into my system as I laid eyes on the photograph of a Noxhelm police car parked in front of the school with the caption, I warned you. My muscles quivered and twitched. My heart palpitated. The office door creaked open, and two uniformed officers entered the room.

"Shana Murphy?"

The counselor squished her eyebrows together. "Can I help you, Officers?"

One of the officers held up a palm to her and then turned back toward me.

"Are you Shana Murphy?"

"Yes, I am."

"Shana Murphy, you are under arrest for the murder of Blaine Walker."

16-TIED WITH A BOW

Upon hearing of Vincent Byrne's death, a marshal showed up at the Noxhelm police station to help my attorney facilitate my expeditious release, and I was out of the boring jail cell by dark. The marshal wanted to come to our house to discuss removal from the program, but my mother was afraid he would discover my father was missing and that he might believe he had something to do with Vince's demise. She fibbed and said he'd been laid up at home with a bad stomach flu, so we all went into an interrogation room equipped with a long metal table and dark-blue, paint-chipped walls.

The marshal with a long, thin nose that quivered at the tip when he spoke opened the discussion. "We've taken over the investigation of the murder of Vincent Byrne."

"So, what does that mean for us? Do we go home to Boston? Are we safe now?" my mother asked as she tapped her fingernails against the metal table.

"Since your family was in the program as a

witness against Vincent, and he's deceased, you are no longer covered in the protection and may move back to Boston. You have thirty days to get your affairs in order. But we've learned you have been charged with murder, Shana. You cannot leave town, anyway."

"So, we're stuck here," my mother said with a somber tone.

My stomach tightened. "Do we keep our fake identities? Can I call my friends in Boston?"

"For now, until the dust settles, it is probably best if you keep your new identity and refrain from contact with anyone in Boston, or any family members you may have in other locations. We cannot protect you from anyone, and with the type of organization that Vincent ran, you don't know what riffraff may want revenge for his death. Not that you had anything to do with it, but they may blame you once they find out your family was living in the same small town in which he was murdered."

I bowed my head, and a tear hit my lap. My mother rubbed my shoulder.

"Do you have any suspects in Vince's murder?" Mr. Nugent asked.

"I cannot discuss the case at this time, but, yes, we have persons of interest. We've had a case open on Vince for years, so we know a lot about him. When your husband feels well enough, we'll need to speak to him, Ms. O'Sullivan."

"Certainly. He's been so sick, he could barely lift his head from the pillow, but I'll call you when he's over it for sure."

An overwhelming sense of dread overcame me, and the reality of my arrest hit me like a piano falling from a fourth-story window. "Can we talk about why I was arrested now? I don't know why the police were so concerned about me being the first one to view Blaine's Yipper post this morning. I was on the app as a guest, just viewing a thread on the Noxhelm High student page, reading about everything that had been said about Blaine's murder. The post popped up, and I took a screenshot of it. So big deal."

Mr. Nugent nodded. "They believe your discovery the moment it posted was quite the coincidence, but they haven't found evidence of you logging in to his account, so they are unable to pin the post on you."

"Can't they find out the IP address of the poster?" my mother asked.

"Yes, they're investigating that, but it may take time. That isn't why Shana was arrested today," Mr. Nugent said.

"Why did they arrest me?"

"They have a witness who says they saw you commit the crime, and they claim a second person will come forth, as well. Coupled with the circumstantial evidence, it's an overwhelming case against you."

"Are you joking? Two people saw me do it? How could that possibly be if I didn't do it? This is crazy! I'm being set up!"

The marshal interjected. "Keep this between us, but as far as I know, they don't have an official statement from any witness. They may have pulled the trigger too soon with your arrest. That's a good thing for you, Shana. Small-town cops aren't used to cases like this, you know."

Someone knocked on the door. The marshal excused himself into the corridor to speak to the uniformed officer. We stared at the door until he returned a minute later. "The police found the castor oil bottle discovered in the trash at the Walker house contains the same oil that Blaine ingested before his death. They lifted the prints from the bottle and did not find your fingerprints."

"So, are they dropping the charges?" Mr. Nugent asked.

"Not yet," the marshal said.

"I heard they found the oil this morning, which I have no connection to, but they arrested me after school? This makes no sense."

"He wasn't murdered with the oil, Shana. You were arrested because they supposedly have witnesses to you committing the crime. We don't know who these witnesses are, and if they have even agreed to come in for statements. Don't worry — your attorney is on the case."

Mr. Nugent nodded. "Yes, I am."

"But the good news is that this evidence points to another possible suspect who had involvement in the crime, which is another step in the right direction for Shana," the marshal said.

"Who?"

"The only prints on the bottle belong to someone by the name of Andrea Clark."

An hour later, my mother and I climbed the steps to our house.

"Give me a hug. I know you need one." She pulled my shoulders in, and I fell against her chest as tears streamed down my face. "I should have never allowed you to be put in this situation. I should have never married someone like your father. I should have moved in with my parents in Salem when I became pregnant with you. I have made so many mistakes, Shana. I am so sorry." Her tears dropped onto my back.

"Mom, you're wrong. You've done everything right. I've had a great life. I love being an O'Sullivan, and I love my father no matter what he does. This is not your fault." I pulled her by the hand into the living room and we sat down on a sofa. "I didn't know whether or not I should have brought up these text messages with the marshals, but I got another one right before I was arrested. I think this person may have had something to do with my arrest."

Her eyes bulged as she took my phone. She stared at the last photo for over two minutes before she shook her head. "We're going to have to tell Mr. Nugent. He can get to the bottom of this." She forwarded the photo to him, and then used her phone to send a text to explain what had happened.

"If Andrea Clark's prints were on the castor oil bottle, and she had a strong motive to kill Blaine, why wasn't she arrested instead of me?"

"He didn't die from the castor oil. The boy died from the knife that was in your hand right after he was murdered."

"But whoever gave him the dose of castor oil is likely to be the murderer, right? The Yipper post proves it, as the picture was of the bathroom before the murder. It was premeditated."

"I'm unsure, but it is suspicious. And it makes sense the two are related. When we left the station, Mr. Nugent was going in for another meeting with the DA to see about having your charges dropped, as everything they have against you — that we know about — is circumstantial."

I turned on the television for some light. "Have you heard from Dad?"

"No. And neither has Mr. Nugent."

"Wasn't Dad next in line to take over back in Boston if something happened to Vince? Do you think he's back there?"

"I don't know, Shana. But what I do know is we are stuck here for now."

I sighed. "For once, I can barely keep my eyes open. I'm skipping dinner and going to bed."

"All right, honey. I understand. See you in the morning."

I climbed the stairs and hurried into my bedroom. After slipping into my pajamas, I turned the television to old cartoons and set the sleep timer. My foot slipped on something wet on the floor, and I nearly fell. I pulled up my foot, and it was bright red, like blood. There was a trail on the floor, out onto the hallway, soaked into the carpet runner. I followed the path to Merry Biggs's room, and in front of her door was a red satin hair bow.

"Mom, come here!" I remained in place with weak knees until she joined me. "There's blood all over the floor — in my room and down the hall." My chest heaved. "Look, a bow. It looks like the same one from my dream that the scary girl was wearing. Do you think Tabatha has been here? She may have killed someone!"

My mother stayed calm and scanned the floor, pinching her eyebrows together. "No, Ms. Gill left earlier this morning and hasn't returned. I don't see anything, sweetheart. Where's the blood?"

I pointed to where the bow had been, but it was gone. My eyes dropped to the floor around me and shifted down the hallway. The blood trail wasn't there. I blinked a few times — there was nothing. My mother sighed and reached for my hand, but I sprinted to my room to find the blood puddle. The floor was spotless. I pulled up my foot, and it was clean.

"It was there. I swear it. It's this house, Mother. This house is not right!"

"Shana, it will be all right. You have been through an ordeal, and the stress is causing you to have a breakdown right now. You've been arrested for murder and were thrown in jail, for Pete's sake. I'll sleep with you tonight."

17—THE LAST STRAW

At 7:15 a.m. on Tuesday, my mother screamed from the kitchen. With my heart pounding, I jumped out of bed and rushed downstairs, still half-asleep.

"Mom! What's the matter?"

With a ruby-red face, she trembled, her eyes glued to her phone. "Ugh!" She showed me the screen opened to my dad's Yipper thread. There was a photo of my dad, Mr. Doyle, Aunt Candy, and a few of dad's former coworkers at his gun range in Boston. "He's smiling. He hasn't smiled like that since the nineties." She groaned. "What makes him think he can just abandon us in this foggy nightmare of a town and go back home to his former life — without even saying goodbye?"

"All right, Mother. Let me play devil's advocate here. If Dad reached out, couldn't it be traced?"

She shrugged a shoulder and tightened her lips. "I suppose it could."

"Maybe this is his plan. Perhaps he hasn't contacted us because it would put us in danger."

"Leaving a damn note on the kitchen counter wouldn't have put us at risk, you know."

"Mom. Remember, you gave Tabatha a key to our house." I smirked. "Dad loves us, and he wouldn't do anything to harm us. Don't draw final conclusions is all I have to say. I need to get ready for school."

During the foggy walk to school, Andrea wouldn't talk about the castor oil, so I had diverted the conversation to something neutral, like how to get a graduation gown since the rest of the seniors had already ordered one. When I had left my classes in Boston, I had only a few grades lacking to complete my courses. Given the easy level of course work in my transfer classes in Noxhelm, I didn't see how I wouldn't graduate with the rest of the class. The day at school flew by, and all anyone could focus on was my arrest and Andrea's fingerprints on the bottle. Many had rallied behind me on social media with the hashtag #FreeShana, but that's how the world usually works—everyone loves the underdog. After lunch, Stephanie pulled me aside to invite herself to my house for a private chat. I told her to come over after school.

The clock turned to 5:00 p.m., Stephanie rang the doorbell, and I answered.

"Hello, come on in." I stepped to the side so she could enter, but she stood still on the porch.

"Um, I—I came over here to see if you wanted to come to my house. Uh, Andrea may pop over, and it will be awkward." She looked behind me with rasping breaths, and I peered over my shoulder but observed nothing out of the ordinary.

"Are you sure? I mean, we're already here. It seems silly to leave to go somewhere else. I don't think she'll come over."

She took a few steps backward. "Yeah, let's go to my house. I'm pretty sure my mother made some after-school snacks, so I'll wait for you on the sidewalk."

"Okay, give me a minute."

I told my mom I was leaving and met Stephanie on the sidewalk. With the dense fog, I was confident Andrea couldn't see us walking down the street. Stephanie lived a few houses down from Blaine, so it was a brisk walk down Moorgate Street, a turn onto Romford Drive, and across the street. The pungent aroma of lemon cleaner assaulted my nasal passageways as we crossed the threshold into the foyer. The house was tidy, not a thing out of place.

"Mom, you home?" Stephanie said as she walked into her living room.

She paused for a minute and then gestured for me to follow her into the kitchen. There were no snacks on the counter. Her mother wasn't home. I found it peculiar she had made such an abrupt switch to go to her house, but shrugged it off. She grabbed two bags of chips from the pantry and two sodas from the fridge. After a brief quarrel with her younger sister about stealing an expensive silk shirt from the laundry room, she guided me to her bright-yellow bedroom with obnoxious sunflower decor.

"It's awful cheery in here." I found a fuzzy yellow chair at her desk and sat down.

"If you can't tell, I love colorful things." She laughed as she hopped on her bed among ten sunflower pillows. "Are you going to the ice cream social tonight? The student council set up a trivia night to distract the students from Blaine's murder. Nobody's allowed to mention the case during the event."

"I didn't hear about it, but it sounds fun. Is it at the school?"

"Yeah, you can ride with me if you want."

I glanced around her room, stopping on her wall racks of brightly colored scarves and the jewelry holders on her dresser with huge bangle bracelets, chunky necklaces, and hoop earrings of every color. My eyes dropped to the ground. This was the topic worthy of a top-secret chat? She gazed at her phone in silence.

"Is everyone invited?" I didn't want another situation with Andrea being excluded. With a murder charge, I had avoided all forms of conflict to keep people on my side.

"Yes, of course, silly."

She handed me a bag of chips and a can of soda.

"So, you just wanted to discuss that?" I rubbed the back of my neck.

She moaned. "Ah, no, I brought you here to talk about this murder case. Like, it's driving me insane." She threw her hands in the air and back down into her lap. "The police are so invasive, you know. I can't sleep, can't eat."

My mouth gaped open. "Excuse me? I'm the one who's been charged with this murder. Hello?" The words left my tongue before I had time to filter them. Stephanie was charismatic, but with an odd quirk that irritated me.

"Shana, we are all well aware you had nothing to do with it." She paused for a strange chuckle. "And Detective Shockley arrested you over an anonymous tip that you confessed to the crime, duh."

I sat upright, wrinkling my brow.

"The evidence against you, as we all know, is circumstantial. It's only a matter of time before the charges are dropped, as the witnesses aren't coming forward."

A flush of energy tingled through my body. "How do you know this?"

"My mother's a cop, duh. Someone called the detective and said they saw you do it, and so did someone else—but then they never came in to give statements like they promised. Technically, you shouldn't have been arrested. Your parents could probably sue the station, ya know."

I drew in the biggest breath my chest could handle, then exhaled. "Wow, that's great news for me. So why are you worried? Why talk to me about it? We aren't really friends, not to be rude."

She took a big swig of her soda and then smiled.

"You're new, and, yeah, I was a jerk to you. I've apologized and admitted I was jealous, so you should be flattered. Believe me when I say I'm not the jealous type. Look at me." She laughed as she gazed into the mirror making a duck-lip face.

"Ha! Flattered that you bullied me? Okay, I guess." I shook my head. Scrambling to find a nice way to say I had to go home, I pretended to view my phone to read a text message.

"They are going through Blaine's devices, his social media apps, the e-mails on his laptop, everything."

"And?"

"I'm going to be honest, but you can't say anything. Do you agree?" She stood up, raising her eyebrows as she gazed into my eyes.

"Sure." With a bogus murder charge, I would have said anything to get information about someone else.

She pulled up a stool next to me and placed her hands on her knees. "Blaine was blackmailing me. I paid him by stealing cash from my mom's wallet, but then I got busted for doing that and couldn't pay for a couple of weeks. I think he maybe told some people about the blackmail, but that's not my concern. What I'm worried about is that the police will think I killed Blaine because of the silly blackmail! Am I overthinking this and being paranoid? Did he ever mention any of this to you? I'm sure he did, didn't he?"

"No, he didn't. What was he blackmailing you for?"

She stood up and walked to her dresser.

"Oh, I mean, it's all stupid, and that's not even what is important. I haven't even mentioned it to my parents because it's, like, no big deal." She watched herself roll her eyes in the mirror. "What matters is that it makes it look like I had a reason to get rid of him, especially since I had just stopped paying!" She marched to her window and gazed outside.

"Who do you think did it, Stephanie?" I asked, beyond curious as to what her theories would be.

"I have two ideas. First, I think it was Andrea Clark. She wasn't invited to the party. She's a Gothic chick, and they're always into death and stuff. She shows up and starts fighting with you, Blaine's new fling—"

I held up my palms. "Stop right there. I wasn't his anything."

She hopped back on her bed. "Whatever, still, Andrea thought that, so it gives her motive. Did you hear they found her fingerprints on the castor oil bottle? My mother said they found a ton in his system, more than just a dose, so he didn't drink it on purpose."

"Wouldn't castor oil just make him poop?"

"Where do you poop, Shana? You do it in the bathroom. Where did Blaine die, Shana? In the bathroom." She flailed her arms in the air. "Maybe Andrea slipped the castor oil in his drink and waited for him in the bathroom? Also, what about the photo that posted on his Yipper account? It was taken in the bathroom before he was killed. Explain that one. If she did that post, she's the killer, period, end of story."

"Good point. Hmm." I stared at my feet for a few seconds. "Who's your number two?"

She slid from her bed and walked back to the dresser to gaze at her reflection as she removed her scarf and switched it for another one on the rack. "Jackie Morgan. Like, I don't want to turn on my friend, but since Friday, she's been distant. Something's wrong with her. She's different." She applied bright-pink lipstick and admired her face. "Well, she loved Blaine and never got over him. They started dating our junior year, and then he cheated on her with that Gothic chick of all things." She paused for a moment and gazed at me with an apologetic expression. "Sorry, she's your friend, and I keep talking about her, no offense. But still, he dumped Jackie without warning and broke her heart."

"Possibly Jackie's just in mourning?" I asked.

She stood back from the mirror as the corners of her mouth downturned and she tilted her head to the side. "I didn't want to say this, but she told me once that if she can't have him, nobody can. I'm not sure what she meant, but still."

A grown-up version of Stephanie knocked and entered the room. Her mother. "Steph, your sister told me you punched her in the throat last night. Is this true?"

"Duh, Mom. No. She's totally a liar." Stephanie rolled her eyes again and watched her face in the reflection.

"All right, can you help me for just a minute? I need you to hold a dowel while I glue it down. It will only take a second."

"I'll be right back, Shana."

The laptop on her desk was partially ajar, so I pushed it open. Thirty minutes prior, she had posted another photo on Yipper of Don and her using a bunny-face filter. I found it strange that since admitting they were a couple, she had posted at least five photos of them with huge smiles on their faces, not appearing as two people who had just lost someone.

My phone vibrated with a text message from an unknown number. My eyes dropped down to view the picture of the front of Stephanie's home with the caption, Confess, or your mother is next. My mind entered a whirlwind. If I told my mother about the photo, she would lose her mind. She had a serious problem with anxiety. If this was a foolish prank, I would stress her out for nothing and the eczema may come back all over her body. On the other hand, if I didn't tell her, and this was a real threat, she would be oblivious she was in danger. I had a sinking feeling the unknown number may have been the murderer. Who else would have an interest in me confessing to a murder I didn't do?

18-ICE CREAM SOCIAL

"Wanna just stay here until the party?" Stephanie said as she came back into her bedroom.

"Um."

It was 6:15 p.m. I still hadn't decided whether I was going to tell my mother about the text, so I needed some time alone to clear my head. I declined and asked her to swing by to pick me up on her way.

"I'll send Andrea a note to offer her a ride, as well. We don't need things getting awkward, you know."

"Yes, I agree."

During the jog back to my house, I decided to show my mother the photo and risk all the ailments she may get from worrying. I figured with everything we had been through with the move, the murder case, and my father, if she hadn't broken out with head to toe rashes yet, she was probably in the clear. When I entered the living room, my stomach turned to rocks.

"Oh, hello, Ms. Gill." I faked a smile. "Mom, can I see you in the kitchen for a sec?"

She held up an index finger. "Shana, in a minute. First, Tabatha would like to tell you something, so please, come sit."

My instincts compelled me to shout and throw things, but instead, I complied.

"Ms. Gill, go ahead and tell her what you heard."

Tabatha gazed into my eyes and waited for my full attention. "Shana, you should stay in tonight. Don't leave the house."

I stood in silence for a moment, then took a deep, calming breath to prevent an outburst. "Okay, is that all?"

My mother cleared her throat. "Shana, Ms. Gill has spoken to Merry Biggs, up in the attic." She raised her eyebrows at me, encouraging me to play along. "Merry said—"

I lost control of myself. "Mother, are you serious? You let this loony tune go into the attic again to speak to a dead girl that doesn't exist? And you're taking the advice from this ghost? Ha! You threatened to call a shrink on me!"

Tabatha sat upright and clasped her bony hands on her knees. This woman had to have escaped from an asylum, and my mother was placating her in our living room. This was maddening. My father would have kicked the crazy woman out of the house.

"Merry has warned against you attending the

school function. Bad things will happen. She says she is sorry for scaring you before, but she only wanted to warn you about her."

"About who?"

"The girl with the colorful scarves," Tabatha said.

"Stephanie?"

"Merry says she is dangerous."

I showed my palms to halt the silly conversation. Tabatha obviously had seen us walking by her house. She may have even been sneaking around the fog and listening to us during the walk to Stephanie's house. She was always lurking about during our walk to school, so who knows who all she had eavesdropped on during the day?

"Mom, really? Are we reduced to this? I'm going to the party. I can't let all the kids from school get together without me there. Even though they aren't supposed to talk about the murder case, we all know they will. If I'm not there, they could all turn on me again, and I can't afford that right now, not until they drop these ridiculous charges. And let me use your words on you—there are no such things as ghosts!" I drew in a steady breath and faced Tabatha. "Listen here. You are crazy. You need to leave. Stop eavesdropping on our conversations. And stop chanting crap and spritzing oils at us from your creepy patio."

A door slammed upstairs, and the lights flickered in the chandelier above us. Tabatha smiled and pointed an index finger toward the staircase.

"Wind draft, old wiring," I said with a sneer. I

wasn't going to allow her to take credit for this make-believe ghost causing the disturbance. I'd been in the house long enough to know it was old and prone to its share of creaks, crashes, and electrical flickers. My mother had convinced me the creepy balloon was a nonissue, so why she was trying to take this lady's side on a paranormal psychic thing, I had no clue. "I'm going to get ready for the social now."

I stormed upstairs, frustrated at my mother for allowing the witch inside of our house again. When I got upstairs, I threw on my clothes, put finishing touches on my hair and makeup, and counted the taffy candy I had left in the bag. Since I'd thrown half the candy away for being melted together, I only had ten left. I vowed to get my life ironed out in ten days, as I'd have no more comforts from home to hurdle me over rough patches.

"Mom, I'll be back in a couple of hours. I need to talk to you about something important when I get back."

She nodded with a wink. At that moment, I realized she hadn't been taking the old woman seriously. If she had believed her, she wouldn't have let me leave the house. Tabatha dropped her head and gazed at the floor.

"Be safe, Shana. Love you," my mother said.

"Love you."

Andrea and I arrived at Stephanie's car at the same time. She slid into the back seat by choice.

Knowing how Stephanie felt about her, it was a nice gesture for her to offer the ride.

We listened to music during the two-minute car ride and then entered the gathering in the high school's gymnasium after taking a selfie at the entrance. There were six chairs at each round table with trivia answer sheets and pens on top. A banana-split buffet was set up on the side of the gym with helium balloons of all colors tied to it and a long line of students in high spirits. The student council president sorted us into groups of six and announced the rules. She warned if anyone spoke of the murder case, they would be asked to stop. I sat down with my heaping banana split at my assigned table with people I hadn't met before. A red balloon from the ice cream table danced around its cohort, but after checking the ceiling and finding an air-conditioning vent above it, I redirected my attention to my ice cream and scooped a huge bite into my mouth.

Stephanie's seat assignment was at a table next to Don, which I'm sure was planned. She laughed as she fed him a bite of chocolate-covered banana and kissed him on the cheek. A violent wave of nausea overtook me for a moment until Lynda stopped by on the way to her table to say hello. The distraction from the lovebirds settled my stomach. I scanned the room, but there was no Jackie. For the next hour and a half, I worked with my team of geeks to answer trivia questions, and they seemed to have vast knowledge about everything from the history of music to quantum physics. My group won the grand prize, which was a catered lunch the last day of school. Even though it was socially awkward to be with a table of strangers, by the end of the night, my spirits had lifted.

I was home by nine fifteen. My mother was asleep on the couch with her sleeping pill bottle on the coffee table. There was no waking her to talk about the new messages I had received. For once, the house was quiet, and I joked to myself about Merry Biggs finally taking a nap. My phone vibrated with a text message. For a second, I considered bashing the thing and never checking it, but my curiosity won. Next in the queue was a picture of me through the window at the ice cream social, sitting at the trivia table. The caption said, You have forty-eight hours to confess. Ironically, this made me feel better. At least we were safe for two days.

19–BY THE TREE

On Wednesday morning, I awoke with a positive attitude. With my mother's premature bedtime the night before, she would be an early riser, so I took the stairs with haste and found her at the kitchen table.

"Good morning, Mom." I took in her gloomy expression. "What's wrong?"

She sat still with her shoulders hunched over, staring into her coffee cup as the morning news blared on the television. I lowered into the chair beside her.

"I'm going to speak to Mr. Nugent about filing for divorce. You and I can move to Florida for a fresh start." She bowed her head. "I owe you."

For a split second, my breathing was suspended. I stared without words until she raised her head. "I don't believe for a minute you want to do that, Mom. We're all under stress. I agree, Dad maybe didn't handle this situation right, but until we get all of the facts, we shouldn't do anything impulsive."

Her quivering lips turned downward at the corner. "Go get ready for school, and I'll make you breakfast. Be ready in twenty."

Deciding it wasn't the right time to bring up the threatening photo, I got up from the table, charged up the staircase, and slid onto the floral carpet of the hallway. I choked as my eyes landed on a girl with a red blouse and a plaid skirt, about thirteen, sitting with her legs crossed on the floor, outside Merry's bedroom. The door next to her was ajar, and she pored over a scrapbook while humming an ominous tune. Her hair was unkempt and tied with a red ribbon. I had seen the hair bow before. After rubbing my eyes, I peered down the way, expecting her to vanish. The sconces on the wall sputtered with electrical snaps and buzzes. She stopped humming and lifted her head slowly to gaze at me, setting the book down beside her. Dizziness overwhelmed me, and black spots infiltrated my vision. The girl stood up. I moved over to the wall to brace myself, as my legs felt like jelly. I followed the direction of her eyes toward Merry's bedroom.

"I want to show you something," the girl said. She had a wraithlike voice.

As if I pushed "Delete," my mind blanked, and I complied with her request. I marched into the bedroom at the end of the hall. From the staircase beyond the small door next to her bed came the soft patters of footsteps up the wooden stairs and into the attic. My feet took me to the steps with a part of my brain shouting at me to rush back down into the kitchen with my mother.

"Shana, I want to show you something." Her voice echoed in the space. She positioned herself alongside the back window, facing the backyard. I grabbed my chest to steady my pounding heart. "By the tree. It's buried there. You'll understand why she did this to me."

With cautious steps, I approached and gazed outside. The girl vanished as if the sun streaming through the window had absorbed her energy.

"What the hell are you talking about? What's buried out there?"

My face pressed against the glass as my eyes darted around, stopping at an enormous fern pine tree on the side of the yard. Dirt surrounded the trunk. I twisted around and surveyed the attic. I was alone. Dead silence. My subconscious told me I would have to fight to keep my sanity.

A steamy shower cleared my head, but I couldn't resist poking my head into the hall to ensure I was alone. I didn't play music or a movie on my iPad, as I wanted silence in case she spoke again, but she never did. It seemed like an eternity had passed before I ended up back at the kitchen table with my mother.

"I need to talk. I don't care if you call a shrink — maybe I need one." I rubbed my temples.

"What's wrong, Shana?"

I told her about seeing the girl and what she had said to me. She stared at her plate for a long minute.

"Maybe you're not going crazy." She sighed. "Tabatha said Merry still lives there. I didn't believe her at first, but she said Merry watched Dad leave the house, and that he kissed both of us on the forehead and then each cheek before he left."

"How do you know she didn't make that up?"

"Because I never told her he left us, and that's what he does when he leaves the house while we're sleeping. I've seen him do it a million times to you." She sobbed and held her face in her hands.

I couldn't fathom how Tabatha would have knowledge of that other than the creepiest possibility that she was present in the room, watching from the shadows. I didn't rule that out. "Mom, it's going to be okay. We just need to get away from this house."

"We can't leave, Shana. Not until they drop the charges against you. You were released on bail."

"I heard good news." She dropped her hands from her face and stared into my eyes. "They'll drop the charges soon. My friend Stephanie said they only arrested me because of an anonymous tip, and the witnesses haven't come forward. The only evidence against me is still circumstantial — what they knew on day one. Her mom's a cop, and she said I shouldn't have been arrested."

"But you were at the scene of the crime, holding the knife. That's enough. They don't need any witnesses to say they watched you push the thing in the boy's chest. They have an excess of witnesses who will say they saw you covered in blood standing over a dead body with the murder weapon across the room."

"Someone slipped him castor oil right before he died, and guess who did that." She stared at me, waiting. "Andrea Clark from next door."

My mom blinked her eyes. "What did she say about it?"

"She won't talk about it, but there's proof she did it. One more thing."

I opened the text thread and handed her my phone, and she scrolled through to the last photo. She slid the phone across the table as she shook her head.

"Don't worry about them threatening me. You know I can take care of myself. But I have spoken to Mr. Nugent about this issue. He said since you didn't bring up these messages from the start, it may appear as though you were hiding them for some reason. Also, with Vince's murder and all, he's unsure if the local police or US Marshals would be savvy that the potential killer knows all about who your dad is, but he said he'd give me the rundown on our strategy. Giving these photos to the police may raise unnecessary questions right when we need things to die down. The account's in Mick's name, so we may not even need to mention the phone. They ask for it, tell them you lost it."

"Mom, what if they've seen me with a phone?"

"We say it was a burner we picked up at the airport because you lost yours. Not to be cynical, but according to the last message, at least we have forty-eight hours."

"They threatened you."

"I said don't worry." She grinned. "Remember how Dad said an associate was delivering guns? The package arrived. We are protected. I'll be fine — don't worry."

"Hmm." I wondered if this was part of my dad's master plan.

Andrea rang the doorbell. I said goodbye, grabbed my bag, and rushed outside into the muggy air.

"Hey, how are you?" I said as I skipped down the steps in the front yard.

Her face was tired, her skin was mottled, and her eyes were puffy. "I've been better."

"What's wrong?"

"The police came to my house last night to discuss what I did at Blaine's house."

We approached the crosswalk, and the dense morning fog made it nearly impossible to see beyond our reach, so we listened for engines as we crossed.

"What did you do?" I said as our feet hit the sidewalk.

She sighed, pinching her lips together. "I was mad, but I didn't kill him. I found out about the party and planned to slip castor oil in the punch bowl to get everyone sick, but there was no punch bowl, only cans. When I saw you and Blaine together —"

"We were not together."

"It appeared that way, and that's what matters. When Blaine wasn't looking, I slipped some into his drink."

"Why?"

"To make him sick, so he'd miss the rest of his precious party."

I shrugged a shoulder. "Okay, I guess I can understand. The police have a problem with that? Seems like a silly prank."

We paused again for the cross guard to escort us across the street.

"There's more." She sighed again. "I snuck into his bedroom after you and I got in the fight. He was in the backyard by the pool, and I believe you were in Don's room with Stephanie. When I opened his laptop, I checked his Yipper app, and he was already logged in, so I scheduled a post for right before school on Monday. Because I'd slipped him a big dose of a laxative, I thought he'd be stuck on the toilet for the rest of the night. It was dumb, I know. After I heard about the murder, I couldn't cancel the post because I didn't know his password. They fingerprinted his keyboard, found my prints, and the IP that the post was made from. Gosh, they can figure out everything, I swear."

"What does this mean for you? They haven't dropped the charges against me, so you must still be in the clear, right?" I secretly yearned for her to say no.

"Blaine's family is putting pressure on the district attorney to press charges against me. I'm not in the clear. The trace evidence analysis is supposed to be completed today. That will be telling, and things may change course in this case."

20-FIBERS

Before the first bell, the tension hung thickly in the air among the students. Frowns, eye rolls, and general irritation plagued the hallways. Teachers seemed under duress and struggled to quiet their classes. The pressure of the investigation had intensified for everyone involved, but I was the accused, not any of them. By the time I entered my final class of the day, news had spread about the trace analysis report, and gossip groups made the room buzz with chatter.

A girl tapped me on the shoulder. "Did you hear about the report? The police completed it. I saw my friend Josh in the hall. He'd just got back from the police station."

"Um, not really." I wondered why this girl I didn't know felt as if she had to share this with me. Did she even realize I had been the one charged with murder?

"They said Lynda Green is no longer a suspect. You know what's funny? My friends and I thought she did it for the money from her great-aunt."

"How do they know Lynda didn't do it?"

"No carpet fibers found on her."

"How are fibers involved with the murder? He was murdered in the restroom, which has tile flooring."

"Oh, well, Blaine showed off his switchblade at the party. Everyone saw Lynda playing with it, and then she gave it back to him. That was caught on one of the videos on Yipper. She never went in Blaine's room to get the knife, so that proves she couldn't have stabbed him. Don saw the knife in Blaine's bedroom on his desk when he snuck in there to steal his binoculars before he was killed. Therefore, anyone without carpet fibers from that bedroom on them couldn't have taken the knife."

My heart sank deep into my chest. I knew what the carpet fiber report would say about me.

In a full panic, I walked home from school and rushed into my house. "Mom!"

She shouted from the parlor, and I scurried through the dining room. She was lying on the red velvet couch, listening to classical music, and reading a book. As if on cue, my phone rang from a number I didn't recognize, but it didn't say unknown, so I was intrigued. I fumbled to put it on speaker.

"Hello," I said as I stared at my mom.

Silence. I sighed, believing it to be a prank call.

"Shana, it's Dad."

My mother stood up, her elbows at ninety-degree angles from her body, her chest thrust out. "How dare you! How dare you take off and leave us here to defend ourselves!" she screamed, her face reddening and veins popping out from her temples.

"Courtney, calm down. My guys are right outside, been tailing you both since I left. I couldn't call until now, as we had to find the moles first. The guys loyal to Vince have all been flushed out. You can come home now. I'm sending an associate over with your plane tickets and some cash."

My heart fluttered.

"We can't leave. Shana's been charged with murder. You'd know that if you hadn't abandoned us."

"Mr. Nugent and I speak daily, and I am aware of everything. I don't care if we lose the bail money. I'm the one who put it up. I sent a dream team of lawyers to meet with Richard. He needed manpower to nip this case in the bud. Don't worry. I'm getting her out of this mess."

"They'll put a warrant out for her arrest if she flees. We're not going anywhere."

"Shana, is this what you want? You wanna stay in Noxhelm? Don't you want to be with your old friends and get away from the fog and that dingy old house?"

I hesitated. I wanted nothing more than to go home, but my mother was right.

"Yes, Dad. But I'll just do things the right way. Today there were more tests that came back against me. I haven't had the chance to tell Mom, but they tested for who had been in Blaine's room. That night they had vacuumed us for fibers and stuff. The murder weapon was in his room, and I was in the room with him before the murder, so I'm sure they found the carpet fibers on me."

"Kid, don't be naive. If you had the fibers, so did the real killer. There's someone who lied to the police, and they'll figure it out. I got people on this — don't lose sleep over it."

My father was the strongest person I knew. He always made me feel better. "Dad, there's something else."

"What's that, sweetheart?"

"Someone's been sending me threatening photos, on the phone that Mickey gave me at the airport. They threatened Mom, and they keep telling me to confess to this murder. The one last night said I had forty-eight hours."

"You kidding me? Give that phone to the associate when he gets there with your plane tickets and cash. I'll have them slip you a burner. We'll get to the bottom of this. No one threatens an O'Sullivan and gets away with it."

My mother rolled her eyes and threw up a hand to mock him.

"Dad, did you take over for Vince?"

She tensed and leaned in so as not to miss his answer.

"I certainly did." He laughed. "We'll be living like fat rats in no time. I can't wait for you two to come home. I love you both. Gotta go—got some pressing business. You can call me at this number whenever you need anything at all. Oh, and by the way, Shana, you got a letter from the University of Texas. They accepted you into the McCombs School of Business. Not sure why you'd want to move there, but that school's got a pretty good rep. Way to go, sweetheart."

A smile spread across my face. UT had been my first choice for the fall.

"Bye, Daddy. Thank you!"

My mom swished her hand at the phone, not wanting to say anything. She covered her mouth and paced across the floor. We sat in silence for more than ten minutes, not knowing what to say about my father's call. I wrote down my dad's number so I could put it in my new phone. The doorbell rang, and my mother answered with a revolver sticking out the back of her pants.

She handed someone my phone, accepted a package, and shut the door.

"Wow, that was fast," I said.

"Shana, they've been here the whole time, and these guys always have multiple burner phones with them." She opened the package, pulled out a phone, and handed it to me.

"That's a stack of cash, whoa."

"Appears to be ten thousand, and here are the plane tickets we can't use." She emptied the bag, folded it, and set it aside.

"Well, I'm going to head to my room, set up my

phone and maybe watch a show before bed. I love you."

"Love you, Shana."

My feet landed on the carpet runner in the upstairs hall. Before I entered my bedroom, I paused to glance at Merry's room. I pondered our earlier exchange and wondered what was buried in the backyard.

21-JACKIE'S
REPRIEVE

At six forty-five on Thursday morning, I awoke to pounding on my front door. I hurried to the door, hoping whoever my father hired to watch over us wasn't sleeping.

"Ah, it's you! What's the matter?"

Andrea Clark stood on the porch, shaking her hands out.

"Can I come up and talk? I'm about to burst if I don't tell someone."

"Sure, come in," I said.

We rushed up the stairs and into my room. I tidied up a bit as Andrea got comfortable in my velvet chair.

"I'm no longer a suspect." She heaved a long sigh.

Instant tears formed, but I quickly blinked them back as I put my dirty laundry in the bathroom hamper. I had secretly and selfishly hoped her involvement would get the charges dropped against me.

"How? Why?" I asked.

"They reviewed the surveillance footage. Cameras point out along the front roofline, and the footage shows me leaving the house before the time of the murder, right after I sent the post from his bedroom. Also, Blaine saw me running downstairs and followed me to the porch and into the driveway, but I was already gone, as I took off. The recording shows him alive at that time."

I forced my next words, trying not to choke on them. "Wow. Well, that's fantastic news."

She shook her head and then stared down at her feet. "Not all good, though. I'm still going to be charged with assault for the castor oil, obviously, and something else to do with the Computer Fraud and Abuse Act. It was illegal for me to schedule the post on his account without his permission."

"Ah, seems extreme, but at least you're not being charged with murder."

The tears surfaced at the rim of my eyelids again, so I crossed over to the window and peered outside at Tabatha's porch.

"Jackie didn't do it; she's also nixed from the list."

I thought I was going to throw up. I coughed and then cleared my throat. "Oh, really?"

"After you and I got into it by the stairs, she went outside, stripped down to nothing, and swam the backstroke across the pool while singing television theme songs. Then she got out of the pool and ate dirt from some flowerpots. Nat Jaylen captured it all on a live feed on Yipper."

"Why didn't this come out sooner if it was online?"

"Nat took the video down immediately after posting because he remembered Jackie's dad's a lawyer. He got nervous with the investigation going on and told his parents about the video. Then they made him tell the cops, and they recovered the deleted video."

"How does this remove Jackie as a suspect, though?"

"There's a digital time stamp on the video and the time places her in the backyard during the possible time of the murder."

I shook my head. "Why'd Jackie do that? Did she drink beer or something? Who acts like that?" With the tears blinked back in their glands, I strolled over to my bed and sat down.

"That's another piece of the puzzle. After Jackie's parents had found out about the video, they tested her for drugs and found Lapse in her system. She doesn't remember taking it, so someone tricked her somehow. Lapse taps into your primitive brain and shuts everything else off, makes you like a shell of yourself, an alternate personality. I guess Jackie's a giant weirdo underneath all that venom."

"Wow, how embarrassing for her, though."

"Oh, and Lynda Green's made an appointment to speak to the cops today with new evidence."

I was gutted. Was she the anonymous witness? Was she going to the police station to give the statement against me? "I thought she was already off the suspect list? What would she have to say now?"

"I'm unsure. The whole thing's strange. Don't you have a class with her?"

"Yeah, we have physiology together. I'll see what I can find out."

Andrea waited for me to throw clothes on, and we took a fast walk to school to catch up on time, as our gossip session had thrown us behind schedule. In English lit, the teacher prepared us for an upcoming exam, and the clock turned slow. My dad sent a text that said his guys were working on the trace for the unknown number. He forwarded me another photo sent to my old phone that warned about the forty-eight-hour mark expiring at 9:15 p.m. I supposed my blackmailer wasn't aware that my father was in possession of that phone. He said not to worry, and he gave me no reason not to believe him.

When the bell rang, I dashed out of class and to my seat, waiting for Lynda to arrive. Jackie wasn't in her seat. Don was back and in high spirits, still wearing the Ace bandage on his wrist. Since I had been accused of his stepbrother's murder, I didn't know what to say to him, but he said hello to me as if nothing had happened.

Lynda ambled into class, staring at the ground in front of her as she marched toward her seat. Her bushy hair had been slicked back into a bun, and she wore a white button-down shirt and black pants — a stretch from her traditional neon attire.

"Everything okay, Lynda?" I asked as she passed.

"Yeah, sure." She took her seat with her eyes facing the teacher.

It wasn't an option to ask her about what she had made the appointment for with the police, so I sat in class feeling the angst of a hundred bees inside a jar.

The remainder of the school day, I couldn't focus on one word from my teachers' mouths, so I spent time perusing my former social media accounts, trying to refrain from breaking the deal and contacting my best friend, Monica. I chose to do what I was told and wait until I was back in Boston to talk to my friends. During advanced health, people were babbling about what Lynda Green had told the police. I couldn't stand it any longer.

"What did she say to the police?" I asked a girl I'd never spoken to before.

She smiled, revealing a mouth full of metal. "Lynda confessed about what she did at Blaine's party!"

"She murdered Blaine?" My heart flickered on and off before it pounded in my throat, forcing me to endure a few hard swallows.

The girl giggled. "No, silly. She slipped both Jackie and Blaine a dose of Lapse. She admitted she was just making an effort to get them back together."

"Was Lapse in Blaine's system when he died?"

"Nope, so he must have caught on to her plan.

Given that he sold the stuff, he probably knew what it was when she tried to sneak it to him. But Jackie's dad is pressing charges against Lynda, even though Jackie's threatening to run away forever if he does. There's so much drama going on right now. This is like a living soap opera. I love it."

"I wish I wasn't such a star in this show. I'd love to be a spectator like you."

"What do you mean by that?" She crinkled her nose.

I sighed. "Oh, nothing."

My eyes drew back to my phone, and I flipped through more posts on Yipper. Then a post from my mother's account popped up on the thread. An upsurge of horror incapacitated me as I read her words. The post said, For those who didn't know — Cullen O'Sullivan agreed to rat out Vincent Byrne. Vince was murdered in Noxhelm, California — the same crap town the feds moved our family to. Is that coincidence? Did Cullen murder Vince to take his place? Who knows, but he's traded his wife and daughter for fame and fortune. Do not trust Cullen O'Sullivan.

22-COMMON SENSE

As soon as the bell rang, I took off toward my house, not even waiting for Andrea to walk with me. I stormed through the front door.

"Mother!"

I wanted to scream at her for what she had done to my dad. I mentally prepared a speech as I searched the house for her, about how terrible it was going to be for me to go back to my old friends with the humiliation of our family business being aired out on social media. I found her sobbing on her bed. Once I saw the remorse in her reddened eyes, I couldn't do anything besides lie down next to her.

"Mom, why?"

Her eyes were swollen from crying. "Shana, I have no clue what came over me. That was the stupidest thing I've ever done in my life. I saw more pictures from our old friends back in Boston with your dad looking happy, and I freaked. I haven't been taking my anxiety medication because I ran out and haven't seen a new doctor here. Look." She held out her arm—it was riddled with a bright-red, scaly rash. "I deleted my post, but people probably took screenshots. I haven't heard from your father. He won't answer my calls. If something bad happens to him, it will be my fault." She grabbed her pillow and threw her face back in it and wailed as loudly as her lungs would allow.

"How long did you leave the post up?"

"About a minute. I regretted posting as soon as I clicked the 'Yip It' button."

Just my luck to be right on top of a scandalous post—but if I saw it, so did others. I did whatever I could to calm her down. It broke my heart to see her upset.

"Maybe I'm the only one who noticed it? Dad's a hothead, and there's no way if he knew that he wouldn't have called you." I rubbed her back until her sobs lightened up. "Hey, I have an idea. Let's invite Andrea over and do a girl's night. We can order pizza and watch a silly teen movie. What do you think?"

"Only if you invite Tabatha Gill." With a forced giggle, she wiped the tears from her face.

"Then it would be rude not to pop up to the attic and invite Merry Biggs." I laughed. "And maybe we'll just watch Casper."

She joined me in a belly laugh, and my heart warmed.

"Oh, you're bad, Shana."

She gave me a hug.

"Love you, Mom. But never do something that

stupid again, okay?"

"You got it." She bowed her head.

"And go to the urgent care clinic and get a new prescription. You know that rash will spread all over your body if you don't stop stressing out."

"I'm going tomorrow morning." She wiped her face and sniffled. "Any good gossip going on at school about the case? Mr. Nugent is working with his new team on getting everything dismissed, but the DA is being stubborn."

I moaned, shaking my head. "Nothing good at this time. Andrea, Jackie, and Lynda are all no longer suspects."

She cocked her head to the side and gazed at me. "Hmm. Whose fingerprints were found on the weapon who hasn't been ruled out?"

"Mine, Stephanie's, and Don's, but they were together in Don's room during the time of the murder, so they have a solid alibi. I even helped them by saying I was there for a time in the room."

"You don't have the whole story, Shana, so don't worry. Tell me the story on Andrea."

I went over the details of why Andrea Clark wasn't being considered anymore.

"Shana, if she killed him, she'd be the dumbest person alive. She scheduled a future Yipper post for the following Monday. That alone screams that she thought Blaine would be alive after the weekend to be embarrassed about the post. Your friend next door's in the clear based on common sense alone, so the video footage that she wasn't there during the time of the murder just sealed the deal." My mother raised an index finger. "Since she's not a murderer, you can invite her over."

She smiled, and I pulled her by the hand to get out of bed.

"Come on — get up. I wanna escape for a few hours and not think about drama. Let's figure out where to order pizza, and I'll send Andrea a text." Then, I remembered my dad had my phone with her number. "Oh no. I suppose I'll have to pop over to invite her, as I don't have her number anymore. BRB."

"What's that mean?"

"Mom, you're so old. Be right back. Oh, order me a Christmas pizza and cheese for Andrea."

I called it Christmas pizza because I liked pepperoni and red and green peppers. I was also a huge fan of the holiday season.

"How do you know she likes cheese pizza?"

"She ate it at school. And who doesn't like cheese pizza?"

In a light mist, I jogged over to Andrea's house and knocked on the door. After about a minute, she answered.

"Hey, you. I'm sorry I didn't wait for you after school, had a bit of a girl problem," I lied. Nobody ever questioned things about a menstrual cycle. "Wanna come over for a girl's night? Pizza and a corny movie with my mom? She needs some cheering up, because, um, she, well, she just needs cheering up."

She shot her eyes to the ceiling for a second and then grinned. "Sure thing, my parents were going out and left me money for pizza, anyway. I'll just leave a note I'm next door." She disappeared for a couple of minutes and came back with a twenty, but I refused to accept it, as my parents had taught me if you invite, you pay.

We topped the steps to my house, and the front door was ajar. Immediately concerned, I surveyed the front yard for my mother, but she wasn't there. I gazed at Andrea and then nodded toward the door. With great caution, I stepped into the foyer. My mother was shouting, followed by a male voice that I recognized but couldn't pinpoint. It was not my father. In a panic, I scanned my immediate surroundings for a weapon but remembered my mother had told me we had guns in the house. She always hid weapons in her underwear drawer.

"Stay in there, and be quiet," I whispered.

Andrea flattened herself against the dining room wall, and I tiptoed up the staircase to my parent's bedroom. I slid my hands to the back of every drawer in her dresser until my hand slid along the cold metal of a pistol barrel. I pulled out an earth-tone Smith & Wesson, checked the magazine, and it was loaded. The sandpapery handle fit snugly into my palm. With a deep breath, I snuck back into the hallway, while running my finger across the indicator on top of the gun. It was slightly raised, and the chamber was loaded. My father had owned a gun range my whole life, so I was familiar with many types of weapons.

After creeping down the stairs, I sprinted into the kitchen, where my mother was arguing with John Patrick Walsh, my father's faux friend and traitor.

"Shana, run. Get out of here—go tell Dad."

With the gun in my hand, I wasn't going to leave my mother with this man. He was standing right by the knife block, so I kept my eye on his hands, pointing the barrel at his chest. Andrea rushed up behind me and gasped for air.

"Shana, what's going on here? Who's that?" she asked.

My hands started to tremble. "A loser, that's who. And he'll be a dead loser if he doesn't leave right now."

"You won't shoot anyone, young lady," John Patrick said.

"Shana, Dad thinks he's dead, so he has no idea. Go call Dad."

John Patrick put his hand on a gun in a holster on his hip.

"Put your hands up, or I'm going to shoot you, Mr. Walsh."

He tilted his head to the side and grinned. "Shana, you won't shoot me."

He continued to grab his revolver and pulled it out of the holster, but my finger wouldn't pull back on the trigger.

"Shoot him!" Andrea squealed.

With a dry mouth and constricted throat, I aimed at his chest, but my hands shuddered.

He pointed the gun at my mother. "Drop the gun, Shana."

Andrea grabbed my hand and forced my finger to fire five shots, landing two bullets in John Patrick's head, one in his chest, and two in the wall. He fell on the kitchen table, streaking blood on it before dropping to the ground. All I could hear was a high-pitched tone for the next few minutes while we stared at one another, catching our breath in the smoke-filled air.

"I'll call the police. You call your dad." My mother reached for her mobile phone on the counter. "Andrea, listen carefully. We don't know this man — never seen them before. Home invasion." My mother studied Andrea with sharp eyes.

"Yes, ma'am, that's what I witnessed. When we got to the house, this dude was robbing you in the kitchen while you were making dinner, and we shot him in self-defense."

"I wasn't making dinner. I was pouring a glass of whiskey."

"Got it," Andrea said in a shaky voice.

My mother called the police, and I sent a 911 text message to my dad's new number. Within a few minutes, he called me back, and I excused myself to the front porch for a private conversation. It was bad enough Andrea was a witness to the fact we knew the dead man in our kitchen. I didn't want to give her more ammo against us just in case.

"Dad, it's terrible."

"The Yipper post, yeah, I know. I've been doing

damage control all day with the boys, our vendors, everyone. I said she had a psychotic break, is delusional, and made up this story in her head. I said she's getting help at a funny farm in Boca Raton. Mickey's backing up my story. You may have lost your tail for a few hours today, but everything's back on track, and we're all in the clear."

"Dad, John Patrick Walsh paid us a visit today. Here, at the house. We shot him. He's dead."

The phone went silent for at least a minute. Then there was a huge crash, followed by a series of expletives. "Dad, you all right?"

"He wasn't supposed to still be with us. He's a dirty rat. I'll take care of this. No worries, Shana, you two will be safe from here on out, as we know who our friends are now. But I do need you to tell me the truth about something."

"Of course, what is it?"

"Since you have moved away from Boston, have you called Vincent Byrne?"

"No, of course not! Why would you ask that?"

"Never mind."

Sirens rang down the street. A police car emerged from the fog and parked in front of our house.

"Any word on the trace? The forty-eight-hour mark is approaching, you know."

"The guys are close. The calls came from Noxhelm. A burner phone. They're trying to track the location now, but it's offline. The moment the snake turns it on, we've got them."

"All right, I have to go. The cops are here."

"Bye, sweetheart. Don't worry about Mom. She's gone through a lot, and I know she's sorry for what she did. Don't be too hard on her."

"Love you, Dad."

Two uniformed officers bounded up the front steps. "We received a call about a home invasion?"

"Yes, please come in."

I ushered them inside to my mother, who was playing the role of a damsel in distress beautifully. Over the next couple of hours, we gave our story of what had happened and waited for the team to come in and pack up the dead body. Using Andrea's phone, I reprogrammed Lynda, Jackie, and Stephanie's numbers into my phone and sent a text message with my new number. I didn't want to miss an important message about the murder case, but more important, I didn't want anyone to be mad at me for not responding to a text message sent to my old number. Until the charges were dropped, I had to be on good terms with everyone. We waited for the county morgue staff to push the gurney into the night air, and then we assembled in the foyer.

When Andrea's parents returned from their date night and caught a glimpse of the police car and county morgue van parked in front, they rushed over with terror-struck faces. Mortified their daughter had witnessed a man getting shot, they demanded that she go home. They grabbed a police officer and interrogated him for the details of what had happened.

Andrea clapped her hands together with a goofy

expression on her face. "It's been fun, guys. We should do it again soon. Next time we should maybe order pizza, watch a bad movie, and refrain from having to shoot psychos in the kitchen, okay?"

We doubled over in laughter until we were in tears, as we were all delirious from the whole ordeal.

"That is a deal," my mother said. "You sure you are all right?"

"Um, I've never shot a guy, but he deserved it. I have a crystal clear conscious, no worries, Mrs. Murphy. It gives me an excellent story to tell my grandkids one day. I think my parents are more freaked out than me." She smiled with an eye roll as she nodded her head toward my front steps.

"Okay, but let us know if you need to talk, or if you need anything at all."

Andrea said goodbye and rushed off into the misty gloom of the night. Mom and I retreated upstairs into her bedroom. She felt it was best if I slept with her, given the excitement of the last few hours. We got into our pajamas and climbed into bed. She switched off the light, and something came to me.

"If Tabatha is all knowing, why didn't she warn us about this?" I asked.

My mother bowed her head. "She did, Shana. She warned me last time she was over here. I didn't listen to her."

23-THE BOOK

I awoke to the young girl standing at the foot of my mother's bed. My first instinct was to scream and wake my mother, but the girl raised a hand to her face, placing an index finger across her lips. Curiosity took over, so I sat up, waiting for her next move.

"I want to show you something," she whispered.

"Are you Merry Biggs?" I asked.

She nodded and gestured for me to follow her into the hallway. She made the motions of walking, but her feet didn't connect with the ground.

"Come."

My mother was sound asleep, so I grabbed my phone from the nightstand and slipped on a pair of flip-flops.

"Where are we going?"

"I want to show you something."

With trembling legs, I followed her down the staircase and into the kitchen. She pointed to the back door and waited for me to open it. She moved to the backyard, turning luminous as if she absorbed energy from the moonlight.

"It's over here by the tree."

"What is it?"

She glided to a spot not far from the tree and then disappeared. My body hairs lifted as goose bumps erupted across my skin.

"I don't understand! What is here? I don't see anything!" In a panic, I got on my hands and knees and felt along the grass. Using my phone's light, I shined the beam across the ground, and there was nothing.

"You'll need this." Tabatha Gill approached.

She wore a white nightgown that cascaded in the gentle wind, and she held a garden shovel. I sat in silence, clutching my phone as I gauged how long of a sprint it would be to get to the back door.

"She just wants you to find it. This will help you." Tabatha stood with the moon behind her, her face as white as her gown. Her eyes were dark as the night surrounding her. I had found myself living the perfect scene of a horror movie.

"What will be helpful? I don't understand what I'm looking for and why I care."

"I'll leave this here for you." She placed the shovel on the ground and walked away.

After careful consideration of whether or not to wake my mother, I decided to press on and thrust the point of the shovel in the exact spot in the dirt where Merry had vanished.

After ten minutes of sweat-inducing shoveling,

the tip hit something plastic. I shoveled around the object and then went a touch further to enable me to get my fingers underneath to lift it out of the dirt. I pulled a large rectangular object from the ground, and then shined my flashlight on it. It was a pink binder. As I held it in my hands, I waited for Merry to appear or Tabatha to return, but I remained alone. The night was peaceful, with owls hooting and insects chirping. I brushed the dirt off the thing and brought it to my room.

"What the heck is this?" I asked myself.

The cover had a huge red heart slipped into the plastic sheath. On the back, another heart. I opened the front cover, and the first page had a low-resolution photo of Blaine Walker's face, printed by an inkjet printer. I recognized the picture from his profile on Yipper. There were hearts drawn with a blue ink pen surrounding his face. I turned the page, and my eyes widened. Someone had cut out Blaine from multiple printed photos and glued them on the page, resembling a strange fifth-grade art project. I turned the page again and saw a sentence written what looked to be more than a thousand times, Blaine will love me. There wasn't a spot of open white space left on the page. After another page turn, I perused news articles cut out and glued to the paper. All were sports updates on the Noxhelm High football team, with Blaine's name underlined with a pink highlighter, tiny pink hearts in the margins.

"Oh, my gosh."

I gasped as I turned the page. There was a photo of Jackie and Blaine at the prom. I could barely tell it was her because there were pen marks all over her with a giant red X across her face. Skimming through the next few sheets, there were more photos of Blaine. My fingers turned the final page, and my lungs seized. It was a wedding scene cut out from a bridal magazine with faces glued on top of the bodies. Blaine's face was stuck on the groom, and Stephanie's was placed on the bride. At the bottom of the page, she had practiced the signature Mrs. Stephanie Walker.

I nearly jumped out of my skin as Merry materialized in my room by the window.

"She did this to me."

"Stephanie? What did she do?" I raised my hands in the air. "I don't know how to say this without being mean, but I heard you killed yourself after you shot up a bunch of people."

"She did this to me," Merry said in an angry voice.

Her eyes morphed into black holes as blood streamed down her cheeks. The trauma from the night's events prevented me from being frightened, and I stood up from my bed and threw the scrapbook in her direction. She disappeared as it slammed against the wall.

"That's it. I'm waking my mother. I'm getting far away from this madhouse."

My phone chimed with a text message, and I opened it as I marched into the hallway. It was another photo from the unknown number. The picture was of me, at the ice cream social, but taken through a window. My face was angry, and I was standing over someone that I didn't recognize. I didn't remember having a conflict of any kind at the event. The caption read, You're unfit for society. It's time for the bars to slam shut.

24-CANDY

Friday morning at five forty-five, I woke my mother and confessed to everything that had happened since we went to bed. After a few minutes, she gave a nervous laugh and cleared her throat.

"Are you serious? You dug this out of the backyard in the middle of the night with a ghost directing you where to put a shovel that Tabatha brought over?"

I nodded. She picked up the binder and opened it to the first page.

"This is the dead boy?"

"Yes."

She studied each page with a grimace. She turned to the final page of the bride and groom, and her hand flew to her stomach. "Who's the girl?"

"Stephanie Evans. Prints on the knife and carpet fibers on her shoes."

"I think I'm going to be sick," she said as she tossed the book aside and darted toward the restroom.

"Mom, are you okay?" I rushed into the bathroom, grabbed a hand towel, and ran cold water over it. My lungs constricted as I gazed in the mirror. Merry Biggs stood over my mother as she sat on the floor by the toilet. Merry turned her head slowly to face me in the reflection. She wore a roguish grin on her porcelain face. I swished around to face her, but she vanished.

My mother climbed to her feet. "I'm fine, Shana." She took an enormous breath and held it in for a few seconds. "Just a bit much to take in, since Tabatha mentioned this book the same day she warned me about all the other stuff."

We shuffled back to her bed. She rested her head on her pillow. I wiped the cloth across her forehead, scanning the room for Merry, but she hadn't returned.

"We have to leave. This house isn't right," she mumbled.

"I've been trying to tell you, but you didn't listen."

Tears streamed down her cheeks. "I just thought the old woman was crazy, but she's been right about everything. She's tried to help, but I've brushed her off. I've failed you. I've betrayed Dad. I'm a terrible person."

"Stop with the poor me bit. You're a strong woman, so act like one. Get out of bed, and let's make a plan."

She blinked her eyes as she gazed at the ceiling,

grabbing the towel to wipe her face. "You can't leave town, but we can't stay here. I can't buy a house or rent another one, because the moment you're free, we're out of this hellhole."

"I can stay at Andrea's until the charges are dropped. She said something in class about her parents leaving for Europe on Saturday. I'll be out of this mess soon, and we're free. You cannot stay in this house alone. I won't allow it."

She clasped her hands under her chin. "I could visit Gran in Salem. It's not too far — maybe an hour and a half flight." Twisting her wedding ring around her finger, she blew out a series of short breaths to gain control. "But I can't leave you in this town. I just can't."

"Mom, there's no other way. We can't stay in this house, and like you said, we can't just get another place. Neither one of us want to stay in this awful town once the charges are dropped — which they will be any day now. Dad has people here watching over me. He said not to worry. Not to be selfish, but it's easier for them to watch only one of us, you know. If I'm at Andrea's, I am just fine. I'll text Dad and let him know the plan. It's the only way this works."

She bowed her head.

"I can't leave you while someone's threatening you."

"Dad will protect me."

"He failed us just yesterday, honey."

"Mom, he admits to that, but it's all good now.

After your social media post, Dad said the guys on watch may have left for a few hours. Who knows? John Patrick probably lied to them or something. What matters now is that everyone's on the same page. Dad's in control. We're protected."

She sighed, sitting upright against the pillows.

"Shana, I just wish I could talk about this with your father. I messed this whole thing up."

"Don't worry. I'll speak to him and see if he agrees. If so, you're going to Gran's, and I'll stay next door. I'll tell him about the pic sent to my new phone. Mom, remember who we are, and he's taken back the reins. We're untouchable, like back in the days when Great-Grandpa controlled everything."

"Back in Boston, maybe, but Noxhelm's another story."

"I trust Dad."

She gave a wavering smile and tilted her head in a side-to-side rhythm. "Let me see the last text message."

I handed her my phone. She maximized the picture, staring at my facial expression. "What are you doing here? You look angry."

"I think it's just a weird shot from the ice cream social. The nerdy event was surprisingly fun, and no drama happened. We played trivia and then went home. Obviously, the mysterious stalker's reaching for new material."

"Any idea who's sending these? I mean, I suppose we made it past their forty-eight-hour mark, huh? Nothing seems to have happened, so this all may be a ruse."

"Yeah, unless you want to say John Patrick fulfilled the forty-eight-hour threat, but that would be a huge stretch to say he had any involvement with the stalker. Especially since they texted me last night with no mention of the dead guy in our kitchen. But, yeah, I gave my number to everyone. Just didn't want to miss an update on the case."

"I agree about John Patrick. Hey, send that new photo to your dad." She shook her head with a heavy sigh. "All right, so back to this book you dug up. Shall we call Detective Shockley?"

I shrugged a shoulder. "I'll let you handle it." I peered at the time: 6:14 a.m. "Maybe give him a bit of time to sleep, you don't want to catch him in a bad mood and cause him to draw the wrong conclusions and think we're being petty."

"I think this proves she had a strong motive, don't you?"

I nodded.

"This demonstrates a severe mental instability." She flipped back through the pages. "She had an unhealthy obsession with that boy. But how do we explain you came across the book? We can't say a ghostly girl told you to dig the thing up in the backyard. That'll come across as insane."

"Um, I can say I stumbled across it in the attic. They're the investigators. They can make sense of it." I paused for a moment. "Why do you think Merry Biggs directed me to this book? Is she trying to tell us Stephanie killed Blaine? Tabatha said

Merry said she wasn't a good person. Maybe this is the she Merry talked about?"

My mother nodded. "Okay, we say the binder was in the attic, and that's all we know." She sighed. "But this Merry ghost thing bothers me, and Tabatha warned us specifically about Stephanie. I can't believe I'm even considering believing this paranormal psychic stuff."

I raised my eyebrows with a smirk. There was no other explanation as to how I would know about a buried binder, and Tabatha's predictions were nearly spot-on. The only thing she had been off on was that I wasn't in danger at the ice cream social.

"Wait," I said. "I heard someone say that Merry and Stephanie's younger sister were best friends. Maybe she'll remember this book? Don't forget to tell the detective."

"Sounds like the little sister may have taken the binder to Merry's house."

"Well, Merry said, 'She did this to me.'"

"Are you thinking Stephanie killed Merry?"

"I guess? But Merry shot a bunch of people at her mother's party downstairs, and then went to the attic and jumped to her death from the circle window. I'm unsure of how Stephanie could be at fault there and how this binder's related."

"You need to tell your father about Stephanie and have the guys watch her, too."

"Will do, Mom."

I sent my father the messages, bringing him up to

speed as I waited for Andrea. Right on time, she knocked on the door, and we set off for school.

"Hey, I need to ask a huge favor."

"Go for it."

"My gran's ill, and my mother needs to go to Salem to take care of her. My dad's gone on business for a while. Can I crash at your place while they're gone? Like, starting Saturday night?"

"Sure thing, but come over tonight, I really want to hang out! My parents are leaving tomorrow. They've been stressing out about the intruder we had to shoot at your house. They almost canceled their trip, and then they said I had to go to my aunt's house in Los Angeles. No, I did not want to do that—she's a cat lady." We laughed. "Then they threatened to hire a nanny and a bodyguard to stay with me. So, I lied and said I was staying with you and that your mother hired bodyguards to watch over your house. That's what those SUVs are parked down the street, right?"

"Um, yes. Of course. Uh, do they not need to speak to my mom? They believed you?"

"Ha! Yes. My parents and I have a trust program. We started it at the first of the year. They took an oath to believe me, and I promised always to tell the truth. Maybe I'm breaking it a bit, but seriously, a nanny? No. I'm an adult. I don't need a dang nanny."

I didn't want to leave my mother alone, so I tried to switch it up.

"Let's stay at my house tonight, then. My mother

flies out early on Sunday, and I don't want to leave her alone. Just don't mention to her that your parents think you're staying here while they're in Europe, okay? Say that I met with them, and everything is set."

"But come over here with me after school so I can pack a fake bag and pretend I'm off to stay at your house."

"Deal!"

"Sounds like a plan, man," she said.

After we crossed Falcon Street, I brought up the unknown texts so I could judge her reaction.

"I didn't mention this before because I thought it to be a silly prank, but I've been getting threatening text messages ever since I moved to Noxhelm. Even on my new phone."

"Are you joking? What kind of threats?"

"They've been sending photos with captions on them. It started as kind of stalking, like, I-can-see-you type things. Then, after the murder, they turned to threats. Whoever this is wants me to confess to the murder I didn't do."

Her mouth fell open. "Maybe it's the murderer? Did you hand this over to the cops?"

Andrea seemed genuine.

"Well, that's the problem. I didn't show them. Now it's like I'm trying to hide something." The photo of the article in the Boston Herald about my father flashed in my mind. Since my attorney was working with the attorney general to prevent my two worlds from merging, I didn't want to open that for discussion.

"What would you try to hide?"

"Nothing, that's my point. The text messages weren't related to the murder at first."

"Shana, I'd tell Detective Shockley. It sounds like this person's the killer, and it could turn dangerous for you. Do you think they sent that man over yesterday?"

I hesitated. "Um, no. Not related at all. Just an estranged distant relative on my dad's side trying to extort money from us. I'm so sorry you got involved in our family's mess."

We stood by the light pole, waiting for the crossing guard at Elm Street.

"Okay, but what you need is for them to arrest the right person. Everyone's at risk while a killer roams free. Nobody believes you had anything to do with it, no worries."

A group of students joined us as we crossed the street, so we slowed our pace once we got on the sidewalk.

"I thought the text stalker was Don. I found binoculars on his desk the night of the party with my phone number written beside it. But they said he took them from Blaine's room, so I'm confused. He doesn't seem the type, and I can't fathom a motive for him to send me threatening texts."

"That's so weird and makes no sense."

"But he didn't kill his brother, so none of it matters."

"Why? Because he was with his girlfriend in his

room? It's clear they'd lie for each other. I have no idea how their alibi's holding up. They both had prints on the weapon and carpet fibers from Blaine's bedroom, and they were right across the hall when someone shoved a knife in his chest. C'mon, it's obvious."

"He got his cast off the same day of the party. Did you see his wrist? He could barely move it, and the bones looked so fragile, they'd probably have broken if he tried to use a fork. He wasn't strong enough to shove a knife through someone's chest. Blaine hated him so much — there's no way he'd let him close enough, either. Plus, I even helped those two with their alibi, so there's no way they'll be suspects."

We approached the school and stepped to the side so we could continue our chat without being overheard.

Andrea lowered her voice. "Stephanie may be the one. She's got a personal trainer, so she's a beast. She could have lured Blaine into the bathroom. The only problem is that I can't figure out a possible motive. I mean, she'd have to be a psycho to commit murder because her boyfriend hated his stepbrother. Plus, Jackie's her best friend, and she's still obsessed with the guy."

"Wait a minute, Andrea. I found something in my attic last night. A binder filled with photos of Blaine and some obsessed ramblings about marrying him."

"Who's binder?"

I halted with a palm in the air until a group of

girls passed, as they had slowed to listen in to what we are talking about.

"Stephanie's! She was in love with Blaine!"

Andrea's eyes lit up like a Christmas tree, and she grabbed me by the elbows.

"No freaking way! I've got to see this—can we stop by your house after school?"

"My mother's handing the thing over to Detective Shockley today. Hopefully, this will turn the case around."

I received a text message from my father as soon as I sat down for lunch with Andrea, Stephanie, and Lynda. I opened the text and leaned back to read it. They live within a block's radius. Keep your enemies close. We're working to narrow down to a house number. And don't worry; I've got your back. Tell your mother to go to Salem.

"Guys, I'm not sure about Don. He's behaved strangely ever since Blaine's murder," Stephanie said as she adjusted her huge yellow hoop earring.

She got my attention. I'd only ever witnessed her and Don being lovebirds.

Lynda choked on her soda and coughed. "You guys have been lovey-dovey lately—what are you talking about? If he's acted strange, it's by the way he's been hanging all over you, Steph."

Stephanie cleared her throat. "Oh, whatever, we've been that way forever—we're dating, you know."

Unable to imagine how Stephanie and Don were

attracted to each other, I couldn't have picked two more different people to be a couple. Stephanie was pretty and over-the-top fashionable, while Don was a nerd with questionable hygiene. To me, their relationship screamed that Stephanie was using him for something.

"Where's Don today? I didn't see him in physiology," I asked.

She pasted on what looked like a fake smile. "Not sure. I think he's sick or something."

I found it strange he hadn't told her why he would miss school.

After school, Andrea and I stopped by my house first to see if my mother had spoken with Detective Shockley and to tell her our plans.

"Mom? You home?" I stepped into the foyer.

"In the parlor."

We hurried to join her in the parlor. She put her book down and smiled.

"Did you speak to the detective?" I asked.

"Yes. He and I had a great conversation. The charges against you will be dropped later today. He's hammering out a few things with the DA, and he'll be in touch with Mr. Nugent's team."

A feeling of breathlessness rushed over me, and I gave her a thumbs-up before clasping my hands to my chest. Andrea grabbed my shoulders with a huge smile.

"So, do they think Stephanie did it?"

My mother continued. "Maybe. I loved how

forthcoming and slightly apologetic the detective was today. He gave me details of how Stephanie Evans dumped Don Walker, the stepbrother, last night for no reason. Then Don called the detective to retaliate and went to the station this morning to offer a full confession that Stephanie had left his room during the time of the murder, and he didn't see her until after you discovered the body."

I gasped for air with my hand flat on my chest.

"She's busted!" Andrea said with widened eyes.

"Don also gave details about how Stephanie was being blackmailed by the deceased about Merry Biggs's death."

"Are you joking?" I asked.

My knees locked, so I lowered onto the sofa. Andrea gave me a cautious grin and did the same.

"The detective told me that Stephanie had confessed to Don that she purchased a couple of doses of Lapse from Blaine." My mother pursed her lips. "Did you know that Blaine sold drugs?"

I exchanged glances with Andrea. "Yes, I found out that night, and that's part of the reason I tried to leave the party. But Stephanie takes Lapse? I thought that makes you go all insane — who'd willingly take that stuff?"

"The detective said teens are using it to film others going crazy and then they post the embarrassing videos online. It's an epidemic for revenge plots, as it can be given in the form of candy," my mother said.

"Wow, that's nuts!" Andrea said. "I had no idea."

My mother continued. "Detective Shockly filled me in that Stephanie admitted to Don that she bought Lapse to sneak to Jackie, so she'd do something terrible so Blaine would break up with her. She told Don she didn't think Blaine, being a drug dealer, was good for Jackie and that she was concerned about her friend. However, the binder tells a different story of why Stephanie didn't want her best friend with Blaine."

I shook my head. "But why would Stephanie admit all this to Don?"

My mother took a breath and quickly exhaled. "Don told the police that Stephanie always talked about finding dirt on Blaine. She knew Don and his stepbrother were at war, so he was an easy way in for Stephanie to get him to help her. Had she uncovered a scandal on Blaine, she could have squashed the blackmail."

"Well, she knew he sold Lapse? Isn't that enough for a counter-blackmail?" Andrea asked.

I pondered the question for a moment. "I watched him firsthand elude a drug sweep at school, so he was smart. He'd just deny it. Second, she bought the drug from him, so that makes her look just as bad."

Andrea cocked her head to the side. "But Blaine broke up with Jackie to date me. Jackie never did anything stupid online until Blaine's party," she said.

My mother nodded. "The day Merry died, Stephanie came home from school and found her younger sister and Merry going through her things.

So the girls snooped through the binder, Stephanie was furious, and there was a huge fight. This incident was all in the Merry Biggs case file. I believe the younger sister mentioned this in her original statement to the police."

"Wait, go back, so Stephanie told Don about the binder, and he didn't have an issue with that?" I asked.

"Stephanie told Don, but she claimed the binder contained silly, embarrassing secrets," my mom said.

"Ah, well, we uncovered the skeletons in her closet, huh?"

"Yes, Detective Shockley thanked me for the piece of the story and was very forthcoming with information. The detective believes that Stephanie threatened the girls, but then later pretended to make up, giving them a peace offering of candy. But this candy was the drug she'd purchased from Blaine that she had intended to use on Jackie," my mother said.

The ceiling shook as doors repeatedly slammed upstairs, and the lights in the parlor flickered. My mother and I gazed into each other's eyes with guarded expressions. Andrea grabbed my wrist and squeezed. I tapped her on the knee and gave her a calm nod.

"It's just a draft in the hallway up there and faulty wiring. This house is so old." I raised a shoulder. "But, Mother, that's terrible! The girls were only thirteen, right?" I said while pretending the disturbance was no big deal.

"Yes. But Stephanie's younger sister didn't want the candy, so Merry ate both of them. The girls snuck away with the binder to have something to hold against Stephanie. They buried it in Merry's backyard and planned to use it as insurance," my mother said.

"So, how'd the binder get in the attic?" Andrea asked.

I gave my mom a wide-eyed look, as we weren't going to say I had dug it up in the backyard.

"Ah, well, I planted some flowers that grow in shade, and came across it. I tucked it away in the attic, and that's how Shana discovered it."

My mother was a terrible liar, but admitting a ghost had told me about it in the middle of the night sounded beyond crazy. I had to remember to keep Andrea out of the backyard because there were no flowers back there.

"Let me get this straight," Andrea said. "Because Merry ate the candy, she murdered her mother and everyone at her party? And then killed herself?"

"Detective Shockley has studied many Lapse cases across the country. The tiniest thing can set you off if you're under the influence, and you do things you'd never do if your brain was functioning properly. I suppose since she was under the influence of a high dose, and being a tiny girl with no tolerance, she snapped when her mother scolded her for digging in the yard during her party. After Merry realized what she had done, the remorse drove her to kill herself."

We bowed our heads for a moment of silence as we thought about the tragedy.

"Did the detective talk to Stephanie's little sister?" I asked.

My mother looked at the clock on the wall. "As I said, most of this information was in Merry Biggs's case file. The detective has record that Cassie Evans had been sent home by Merry's mother when they got in trouble for digging in the backyard. There was no mention in the file about why the girls had been digging. Since Stephanie's little sister wasn't an actual witness to the tragedy that occurred, her interview transcript from that day was brief, and there was no mention of a binder or the candy Stephanie supposedly gave them. Detective Shockley's probably talking to her now, though, so let's hope she remembers everything from that day. Stephanie's likely to deny giving them candy and making that binder. Since the book was discovered in this house, there may be a snag, and it could even backfire on you if she makes a claim you're trying to frame her. But after Cassie corroborates the story about the binder, he's filing the official paperwork to drop the charges. Stephanie's fingerprints were on the knife, and she had Blaine's carpet fibers on her shoes. Don no longer gives her an alibi, and she had a strong motive."

"It doesn't look good for her, that's for sure."

25-WORLDS COLLIDE

My phone rang at 9:45 a.m., and the ringer was set so high, a brief squawk unleashed from my lungs. With a pounding heart, I answered the call. "Hello."

"Sweetheart, we got the address — 515 Romford Drive. Who lives there?"

"Andrea." I scooted over to her sofa and shook her shoulder back and forth until she opened her eyes. "Hey, who lives at 515 Romford Drive?"

It seemed like an eternity passed as she rubbed her face and cleared her head.

"Hold on, Dad — I'm finding out."

She moaned and sat upright. "Um, Blaine's at 512, so across the street and one down would be Stephanie Evans."

My heart dropped into my stomach. "No way. Dad, her name's Stephanie, and she's a girl from school."

"Already sent the boys over to the address. Nothing to worry about now, sweetheart. Mr.

Nugent says they're about to drop the charges on you. I've got your room ready with clean sheets, the fridge stocked with your favorite treats, and I've hired a planner for your welcome-home party. She's not invited anyone yet because she's waiting for the date."

"Dad, don't send anyone to that address!"

"Honey, nobody messes with an O'Sullivan and gets away with it. I'll see you when you get home. Love you." He ended the call.

"What's wrong? What's your dad going to do?"

"Oh, my gosh." I rubbed my head and bit at my lip. If I told the truth, my father would be implicated with whatever his guys did to Stephanie or her family. I calmed myself and came up with a cover story. "Um, he said he was going to send attorneys to her house to serve civil suit papers against her parents for not disclosing — well, you know, the story." I was scrambling, and my words weren't making sense. I had needed a diversion before I dug myself further into the web of lies. "The television, it was on a sleep timer! Turn it back on and check the news to see if anything's going on with Stephanie. I have to speak to my mom. I'll be right back."

I rushed upstairs and woke my mother to give her the update, leaving Andrea downstairs to watch the news.

"Mom, Dad found out who the stalker is, and it's Stephanie, from down the street."

She squinted her eyes as she propped up on pillows on her bed.

"You serious?"

"Yes."

"Well, that makes sense, given she's most likely Blaine's murderer. But how did she get your number right after we moved here? I remember you said you got a text soon after we got in town."

I tried retracing my steps on my first day in Noxhelm. I had given only Andrea my number, but I quickly found a possible scenario. "I gave Andrea my number the day she came over to help me pick my bedroom. The night of Blaine's party, I saw my number written on a scratch pad in his stepbrother's room. Andrea was secretly dating Blaine at the time, and when she left our house, she must have gone over to Blaine's. Stephanie was probably there with Don. Maybe she overheard Andrea talking about me and sneaked my number from her phone—who knows? Their rooms are side by side—anything could have happened for her to get my number."

"But why would she send all those messages? How did she know about Dad?"

"If she killed Blaine, which it appears as though she did, she's a psychopath. You saw the binder— she's nuts! There's your reason. As far as how she knew about Dad, there's many ways for her to have found out. I gave a big lead the night of Blaine's party. I lost control. I said something along the lines of my father being a dangerous man. I can't even remember what all I said, to be honest. I kind of blacked out I was so mad. And with today's technology, she could have put a picture of me online, found a match, and connected the dots. There's many ways."

"She's probably the anonymous witness, huh?" my mother asked.

"Most likely. She knew I was a suspect due to circumstance, and if she could pressure me into confessing to something I didn't do, she'd be in the clear. Ugh, the whole thing's so pathological. She pretended to be my friend. Well, I'm going downstairs with Andrea to watch the news. We're waiting for her to be arrested. Can't miss it."

She slid out of bed. "All right, honey. Love you."

My feet took the stairs with haste. Andrea's eyes were glued to the newscast and she had a frown on her face. The reporter was talking about a summer festival coming to town for the next weekend. Police sirens rang in the distance.

"Holy crap, they're coming now," I said. "We should go watch, huh?"

"Yeah, let's go."

We threw on our shoes. As we were hurrying down the front stairs, Andrea got snagged by her parents over in her driveway. The taxicab had come to take them to the airport. By the time they gave her the list of last-minute instructions, the police had parked in the street on Romford Drive. We could barely see the red-and-blue lights through the fog. Andrea's parents were running late, so I was glad they didn't get caught up with what was happening down the street.

"Run," Andrea said after the taxi pulled off into

the fog.

We tore off toward Stephanie's house and ducked behind a bush across the street. I snapped a photo as she was being escorted into the back of a police car with her parents shouting at the officers along the way. There was a local news truck in her driveway, filming the scene, so we made sure to stay out of sight. A black Cadillac Escalade pulled toward the house, paused, and then drove down Romford. I was elated. My father's guys were too late.

"That was insane. Let's go watch on TV and see what they're saying about it," I said, tugging on Andrea's sleeve.

We jogged back to my living room and turned up the television. The arrest had taken over the newscast. The reporter revealed the charges had formally been dropped against me. I bit down on a smile as my insides vibrated with an energy rush. Andrea held her hand up for a high five. The newsperson went on that Stephanie Evans was being arrested for the murder of Blaine Walker, and an inquiry was being opened into Merry Biggs's death.

Andrea and I launched into an all-day gossip session about possible scenarios of what would happen to Stephanie. We followed every comment on social media from the kids at school. Later that afternoon, my mother pulled me into the parlor for a private conversation.

"I'm beyond thrilled that you're in the clear. Here, take this." She handed me an envelope.

"That's a ticket home, and the car will pick you up from Andrea's at ten a.m."

"But why won't you come with me? If it's all over, and we can leave Noxhelm, why not just switch your ticket to Boston?"

"Honey, I believe you know the answer to that. I'm going to take some time, visit the family in Oregon, and we'll see where time takes things. I haven't been happy with your father for quite some time, and you're going off to college in a few months, so there's really no reason for me to go back. Before Mr. Flynn attacked him, I had just convinced him to get out of the whole underground thing, and now he's back in it as the ringleader. That kind of life isn't for me, or you, but it's the safest place for you to be for now. I've been on the phone all day and worked it out with the school. They'll put you right back in your classes so you can graduate with your class, right next to Monica like you always planned. You'll have to attend Saturday school for two weeks, though."

With tears in our eyes, we hugged. The doorbell rang, and I rushed to the front door. After peeking out the peephole, a sour taste formed in my mouth as I opened the door for Tabatha Gill.

"Shana," she croaked. "May I speak with you?"

I waved off Andrea, stepped onto the porch, and shut the door behind me. I didn't want Andrea hearing any of her paranormal predictions, as that would launch a whole new discussion that I didn't feel like having.

"Um, as of tomorrow, I won't live here anymore. You have the key, so you can live here until they kick you out for all I care."

Tabatha wore a grim expression. She raised her chin. "Shana, you will soon learn the truth."

"Uh, yeah. Stephanie killed Blaine and Merry. I get it."

"That is not the complete story. Merry tried to save you from your fate, but she failed." She gazed at me, and I waited for her to continue. "Shana, you'll be faced with a dark reality soon. When it comes, remember to hold on to the light and don't let it go, or you will be in for a life of despair."

"Oh, okay. Thanks."

With shaky limbs, I spun around and went back into the house to join Andrea on the couches.

"What was that about?"

"She wanted to hang out with Mom, but I told her what's up," I said with a laugh. I wanted to void the chat with Tabatha from my mind and enjoy my newfound happiness of going back home and being free. "So, guess what!"

Andrea smiled. "Chicken butt?"

We laughed for a moment. "My mom bought me a plane ticket to visit my dad tomorrow morning."

"Really? Didn't you say he was in Boston for work? What about school? How long will you be gone?"

"Um, yes, going to Boston." I hated goodbyes, so I didn't want to admit I wouldn't be coming back and figured I could stay connected through social media once I got home. "Uh, I'll just miss a few days. I'll study for finals while I'm gone, no biggie. Will you be okay at home by yourself? I hate to leave you."

"Girl, I'm eighteen—are you serious? It was the plan from the start—my parents just started tripping over that dead guy. We both know he came here because he was mad at your family for whatever reason, so I'm not in any danger. I'm fine."

Within minutes we sank back into the routine of following social media feeds about Stephanie's arrest and the Merry Biggs case. My phone rang, and I answered my father's call.

"Sweetheart, do you remember the bag of candy from John Patrick at the airport?"

The question caught me off guard. "Yeah, that bag of taffy, from a local Boston candy—"

"Have you eaten any of it?"

"Um, yeah, I've eaten like half, maybe ten pieces. Some of it got melted together, though."

"And you feel okay? Nothing happened?"

"Yes, Dad. What's the matter with it?"

"Mickey and I went through everything that snake had done since this all started. I can't believe he turned on me; we've been friends since we were kids. Throw the rest of the candy out. Do not eat another piece."

"You're scaring me. What's wrong with it? It's poisoned?"

"We're pretty sure it's dosed with Lapse. He did it to get even with me for turning on Vince."

"So what does that mean?"

I listened intently to what he said. Andrea stared at me with concern riddling her face. I pulled the phone away for a second and told her the candy might have been part of a bad batch, but no big deal because I felt fine.

"Remember when I asked if you had contacted Vince?"

"Yes, and there's no way I'd ever do that."

"You do not remember calling him?"

"No, of course not!"

"I'm not angry, but I know you called Vince. We have the phone, sweetheart, and the calls are on record. You spoke with Aunt Candy. And twenty minutes after that, you called Vince and spoke to him for over fifteen minutes. This was three hours before he boarded the plane to California. You also chatted with him the night he was murdered."

"But, Dad. How could I —"

"You're not in trouble, sweetheart. Aunt Candy told us everything. She said she only got with Vince because she wanted revenge for what he did to Uncle Cillian. Vince killed your uncle so Aunt Candy would have no choice but to be with him. She told me the whole story of how she helped you set it all up. We've destroyed the pictures you had on your phone of Vince's body, so don't worry. I'm not mad, Shana. In fact, I'm deeply in your debt."

"No. No way. There's no way," I paused as I realized Andrea had her ears pinned back, hinging on my every word. "Um, Dad, there's no way I would ever forget Aunt Candy's birthday. Tell her I'm so sorry, and I'll make it up to her when I visit for the holidays."

26–THE HORROR WITHIN

A daze took hold of me for the remainder of the night, and my happiness turned to hopelessness. I needed quiet time alone in my head to sort things out, but Andrea was at my house, and I didn't think I could get away for the length of time it would take to speak to my mother about this issue.

"Hey, let's watch a movie. Maybe a marathon of Lord of the Rings?" I asked.

She smiled. "How did you know that's my favorite series?"

"Duh, me, too. Wanna start with The Fellowship of the Ring or do you want to do The Hobbit movies first since they're prequels?"

"The Hobbit."

"Got snacks?"

"Of course, silly!"

We quickly grabbed sodas and bags of snacks from the kitchen—the smell of bleach and bad memories was enough to drive us away from there. After taking our spots on the sofas, I pushed "Play," and the opening credits blared. I pretended to glue my eyes to the TV as I shoveled popcorn into my mouth. Unable to process that memory-loss drugs had morphed me into an alternate, murderous version of Shana with her own set of motives, I was forced to face that it was possible I was a cold-blooded killer. This was a crushing reality, even if it was the man who killed my uncle and would've executed my father if given a chance—if not our entire family. As the movie went on, I turned catatonic with thoughts racing through my mind. Had I orchestrated a plot to murder my dad's boss while under the influence of this drug? The evidence against me was formidable.

To my best recollection, the first piece of candy I consumed was on the plane to California. Thinking back, after the turbulence hit, I didn't remember much, as if my mind had deleted the footage. The rumor going around Noxhelm High was I hooked up with Blaine in the lavatory of the first-class cabin. They called me Easy-Breezy Murphy, which is a peculiar nickname to make up out of thin air. But did I do that? I hadn't collected the memory, if so. I reached for my phone but then realized my father had the one from my first days in Noxhelm. I always took photos of everything, so I was humiliated to think of what he'd seen on my camera roll. I kicked myself for never viewing my pictures, but since I wasn't posting to social media anymore, I had no reason to check them out. I had taken them to show Monica when I got back to Boston.

I strained to remember the night of Blaine's murder. Throwing myself back in the night, I traced the events as I stood over the dead body in the restroom, peering over at the guy from school as he said, Why did you kill him, Shana? Because he told everyone what you guys did on the plane? I gasped, holding my palm against my chest. Instinct forced me to my feet to prevent a cellular implosion.

"What's wrong with you?" Andrea asked.

"Nothing, just a panic attack, I'm gonna walk it off." I marched around the living room. "I'm going a bit nuts because I've been eating a bad batch of candy that might have been contaminated with salmonella."

She used the remote to pause the movie. "You haven't eaten any candy today, and salmonella gets you within six or so hours, makes you real sick. Don't worry."

"Yeah, you're right."

After I had lowered myself on the couch, she switched the movie back on, and I struggled to recollect the ice cream social but kept drawing a blank after the first round of trivia up until the moment my team won the prize. The ride home was missing, as well.

"Can I ask you something?"

She stopped the movie again. "What's up?"

"The night of the ice cream social. Um, did anything strange happen?"

She chuckled. "Oh, so you finally want to talk about what happened between you and Prashanti Patel?"

With a false smile and restless legs, I responded. "Yes."

"Don't worry, Prashanti's not mad anymore. Nobody can stand her, anyway. But I have to admit, you acted a bit psycho over a stupid Harry Potter trivia question—don't you agree?" She laughed.

I shifted, unable to get comfortable. "Um, my memory's kind of fuzzy for some reason. What exactly did I do?"

She laughed again. "There's no way you don't remember marching across the gym, taking her banana-split bowl, and dumping it in her lap while you screamed at her for cheating." Another bout of laughter. "C'mon, you remember that. No way could you forget. Then, after you got an in-school suspension from the vice principal, you and I walked home because Steph took off with Don. You ranted about her all the way home." She snorted.

"Oh, really?" I forced a smile.

"You don't remember?" She brought her eyebrows together.

"Oh, um, yes. It's just fuzzy."

"Ah, well, I'm sure you recall Prashanti admitted she cheated with a second phone, so you were in the right, nevertheless. You remember now, huh?"

"Oh yeah, I do. Just wanted to catch your take on what happened since we haven't spoken about it. I'm silly sometimes," I lied.

There were zero memories of the Prashanti incident, being punished with a suspension, or walking home with Andrea. I'd eaten the candy before I got into Stephanie's car. At least I hadn't harmed anyone or done any significant damage that night.

The movie droned on, and I hurled my brain back to the night of the murder and traced my actions. The memories faded out after I left Don's room. Did I find the body? Or did I kill him? I had motive, opportunity, and had seen the weapon. All I could remember was removing the blade from his heart and throwing it across the room. My memory was two reels smudged together with adjoining pieces that left out an important chunk of the story.

"Hey, I'm gonna talk to my mother about some stuff since we're both leaving in the morning. Just wait here and finish the movie, I'll be back in a bit."

"Seriously, Shana. You okay?"

"I'm good. Thanks, just stay in here. Sorry!"

I crept upstairs and knocked on her door. "Mom!" I waited for her. "Mom, I need to talk."

"Come in," she said as she put her book down on the end table.

She patted her hand beside her, and I climbed on the bed and took my spot. I clasped my clammy hands together and bowed my head. "I killed Vince. I might have also killed Blaine."

After leaning up to check if the door was shut, she cleared her throat. She cast a stern gaze into my eyes. "What? Are you crazy? Why would you even say that?"

Sudden heartburn erupted, and I pulled at my hair, twisting it around my index finger. "I'm serious. You can talk to Dad later about the Vince thing, but it's pretty apparent I did it with Aunt Candy's help. Don't worry—he's destroyed all evidence, and I'm in the clear."

Her posture stiffened as she sat up. She shook her head no.

"But there's more. As far as Blaine's murder, I'm just now putting it all together. Dad said John Patrick put the drug Lapse in that bag of candy from the airport. I've eaten over ten pieces. There are blank patches of time where I have no clue what I did. Mom, if the evidence against me fits, it might be true."

She crossed her arms over her chest, shaking her head back and forth. "Stephanie was arrested. There's compelling evidence against her, end of story. Listen to me, Shana. Never repeat what you said again."

I grabbed her hands and squeezed. "There may be a chance she didn't do it. The evidence is just as circumstantial as the evidence against me."

"Shana!" Andrea shouted from downstairs.

I jumped off the bed. "Hold on, Mom. I'll be right back."

With the sconces on the wall flickering, I rushed down the hall and took the stairs at full speed. Andrea was waiting in the foyer, bouncing from foot to foot. She was shaking and twitching all over.

Winded, I huffed for air as Merry Biggs approached from the dining room. She held a red balloon by the knot. My eyes darted between her and Andrea, but Andrea was unfazed. Merry gave a sorrowful frown and bowed her head.

"Shana, you'll never believe what happened!" Andrea said.

I gripped the stair railing with eyes glued to Merry as she lifted her hand holding the balloon, tears of blood streaming down her face. She let go, and it soared into the air and vanished before hitting the ceiling.

"Shana?" Andrea tried to get my attention — I must have appeared to be staring into space.

Merry waved goodbye. She glided back into the dining room. Andrea looked over her shoulder to see what I was gaping at, but with a confused expression, she shot her eyes back at me. I shook out of the trance and gazed at her. "Spit it out! What?" I asked.

"Lynda Green just called me. Stephanie's been released, charges dropped."

Every cell in my body tingled. I held my breath without a word.

"Don was forced to confess that he lied to the police about Stephanie leaving the room during the time of the murder. He said he did it to get revenge on her for using him to get close to Blaine. The investigators uncovered a hidden camera from his room that had filmed him and Stephanie in his bedroom the entire timeline of the murder. Not only was she the one who retrieved the binoculars from Blaine's room; she never left the room until after the body was discovered."

I exhaled. My stomach hardened, and I lowered myself on the bottom stair.

She cleared her throat and lowered her head as she stared at her feet. "Well, it also time-stamped you, Shana. They have the exact time you left Don's room, and it's only eight minutes before you discovered the body—which happens to be only a minute after Blaine's caught on camera running after me in the front yard."

The police sirens rang in the distance. A grave feeling took hold that they were going to stop in front of my house. I wanted to run and hide, but my muscles turned rigid. "So what does this mean?"

"Shana, I don't know how to say this, but—"

My mother descended the staircase with an incredulous gaze as the red-and-blue lights flashed through the window. The door creaked open without anyone touching it, and the fog crept inside as footsteps pounded against the concrete steps.

"You don't have to say anything else, Andrea. I already know."

I got up from the stair, grabbed my shoes from the foyer, and slipped them on.

27—THE GRIM TRUTH

"Shana, you cannot skip dinner again," my father shouted from downstairs.

"Dad, I'm not hungry. I've told you a thousand times. I don't need three meals a day!" I shut my bedroom door and plopped down on my white leather platform bed.

Not long after I was arrested for the murder of Blaine Walker for the second time, my legal team negotiated house arrest for me in Boston. Six months later, I had sunk into a mundane, maddening routine and started to go stir-crazy. The majority of my close friends had left for college by the time I arrived in my father's new home. Day in, day out, I attended my online course lectures and spent hours on my homework. The chef prepared breakfast at eight o'clock, lunch at one, and the daily debate about dinner started at six. My video chat with my mother was the highlight of my day after my trainer left each evening. I loved to hear about her flourishing in Oregon. She'd opened a clothing boutique like the one she'd had before she met my dad. She was two dates into a budding relationship with a chiropractor she knew from elementary school, and things seemed promising. My parents' divorce had been fast-tracked, but both of them appeared to be better off, which made me happy.

About a minute later, my father knocked on the door. "Shana, can I please come in?"

I sighed. "Yes, Father."

He switched on the light that lit up the main chandelier and the pink LED lighting around the bed.

"I apologize. I just don't need to eat that much. I love you."

"I love you, too, but I'm worried about you, sweetheart. You've been moping around the last few weeks. Chef Bobbi said you're not finishing the food on your plate. I think the stress of being in this house is getting to you. There's one more semester of online classes and then, the summer, and you'll be in your new dorm in Texas."

"Dad, this is a beautiful seven-thousand-square-foot house. I'm not moping—how could I?" I lied. I was losing it, but he had a point that I was halfway through my punishment, and it lightened my spirits.

"I have a surprise for you. You ready?"

Perplexed, I sat up in the bed, and a smile spread across my face. "Sure, what is it?"

Andrea Clark emerged from the hallway with a grin lighting up her face. "Surprise!"

"Oh, my gosh! I just talked to you last night. You

sneak!"

Her chestnut hair had grown to one length with a cute upturn at her shoulders. She wore pastels with a hipster vibe; her Gothic past had been erased from her appearance in every way.

We laughed and gave each other a long hug. "Your dad's attorney helped me get permission to leave town. We've been trying to set this trip up for four months!"

"Dad, thank you! You're the best!"

"You're welcome, sweetheart."

She sat down on the bed. I grabbed her hand and squeezed with a smile. We had kept in touch, but our attorneys had given us strict orders not to discuss either of our court cases over the phone or online.

"How much longer are you on probation?" I asked.

"Oh, man. It seems like forever, but I've already calculated it will be two months after my twenty-second birthday. I was found guilty for my involvement in the castor oil and computer-hacking incidents. The Noxhelm judge showed no mercy."

"The district attorney's mean — I feel ya."

My dad knocked on the door to get our attention. "I'll leave you two to catch up. I'm sending Chef Bobbi up here with your dinner trays. Since you wouldn't come downstairs to eat with Andrea, you'll be dining up here."

We giggled as he left the room. She stood up from the bed and ran her fingers along my textured wall.

"This place is amazing!"

She strolled onto the marble floor and then pulled off her shoes to run her toes through my charcoal shag carpet in the center of the room. After taking in my decor, she came back to the bed and sat down.

"Thank you. My father decorated it for me."

She leaned in for a big hug. "So, how have you been? How's school? It's been so frustrating not to talk about what happened with our cases. The kids from school have posted all kinds of things from you being in prison to walking away without a penalty. Everyone thinks they know something, but nobody knows anything." She chuckled. "I've been dying to hear what happened with you. Since your attorneys settled and there was no trial, all I heard was that you didn't go to jail and moved away to Boston. I see you're wearing an ankle monitor."

"Yes. This thing's driving me nuts!" I tugged at it. "I'm doing online courses for my freshman year of college since I can't leave the house. I'm like a caged rat, but I'm making progress. Time's passing."

"This mansion's unbelievable. You have a courtyard with a garden in the front—seriously, who has that? I can't imagine what your backyard is like. Shana, please let me get stuck here with you."

"I should be thankful I get to spend house arrest in a place like this, but it's still nerve-racking not to step past the property line."

"Can we take a tour? Please? I want to see the backyard first!"

"Yes, I don't want dinner, so let's scoot before

Chef Bobbi delivers it."

We laughed as we sneaked down the corridor and the spiral staircase.

"Not to dredge things up, but how in the heck did you not go to jail? Is it true you murdered Blaine? Like I said, some of the posts online say since you have all this money and a powerful dad, you got away with murder."

I opened the door to the backyard, and we strolled out onto the enormous terrace surrounding the swimming pool. Four massive columns lined the circular patio with marble statues of lions positioned in between them facing the water.

"This place is to die for."

"Thanks."

We walked to the edge of the pool and stood by the water.

"All right, to answer you about my case. I'm not offended — it's a valid question. We believe I killed Blaine, but we don't know for sure. Had I gone to trial, it wouldn't have been an easy case for the DA, as we had enough proof for reasonable doubt I didn't do it. But Mr. Nugent and his team worked out a deal to duck a trial because it's always best to avoid one."

"That's good, right?"

"Yes, it was for the best. It was my first offense, and I was involuntarily under the influence of a synthetic narcotic — that Blaine gave me, by the way. Also, it was determined to be self-defense. Blaine's parents fought to keep the recordings of his last minutes out of the public eye to save face for their family and not tarnish his reputation. This helped sway the DA, as well."

"What? Recordings exist? How?"

"Don secretly filmed inside of Don's bedroom while he and Stephanie were in there that night. I don't know why he did it, but still."

"Yeah, it's strange. That was probably the last thing he ever wanted them to find, but that's what got Stephanie off."

I motioned for her to sit with me on the loungers under the thatched gazebo by the pool. Sheets of water flowed from fountains into the pool. A cool breeze blew through, so I grabbed two heated blankets from the stand and handed one to her.

"Here comes Chef Bobbi with our trays."

I moaned and pushed my chair into an upright position as I covered my legs with the blanket. Andrea did the same.

"Good evening, Miss Shana. Your father said you'd be dining by the pool, so I brought you out a special poolside drink to enjoy with your dinner. It's a pineapple coconut punch, quite tasty and refreshing. I've turned on the pool heater if you two want to swim."

"Thanks, Bobbi."

He finished setting up our dinner trays of shrimp scampi, spinach salad, and roasted potatoes. Andrea's eyes danced in delight at her plate. I tasted my punch. He was right; the drink was yummy.

"Okay, so, my dad hired a team of forensic audio

engineers to research if any other voices could be heard in the hallway during the time of the murder. The guy found gold. He picked up audio of my voice screaming for help. Blaine attacked me, and that's when I must have stabbed him. It was determined to be self-defense."

"Oh my. I can see why Blaine's parents wouldn't want that getting out. But if it was self-defense, why do you have to wear the ankle bracelet?"

"It was the deal we made to avoid a trial and for them to keep it off my record. Blaine gave me the chocolate laced with Lapse. My attorney made a case he did it on purpose. But I took the knife from Blaine's bedroom and ended up in the bathroom with him. I didn't start screaming until we were behind closed doors. Had I shouted for help in the hallway, she wouldn't have slammed the bracelet on my ankle. So I might have lured him in there while hiding the knife — we'll never know."

"I didn't realize Blaine gave you the Lapse that night. I heard another rumor you'd been unwillingly taking Lapse since your arrival in Noxhelm, like from the tainted bag of candy? Maybe the candy that you were worried had been contaminated with salmonella?"

"Yes. The bag of taffy was given to me laced with Lapse. Actually, you met the guy that gave it to me — we killed him in the kitchen."

"Oh, gosh. That was who gave it to you? That sucks. Now that I look back, I can guess when you were on it, as sometimes you seemed like a different person."

I took a bite of spinach salad and shook my head. "I'm so embarrassed. You'll never know how it feels to have two personalities living inside you with one taking over your body and doing whatever she wants. Then, when you're back, you have to own up to whatever she did. It's humiliating."

"No worries, Shana. They say there are no long-term effects after a few months. You're in the clear now. We've all learned a big lesson not to take candy from strangers!"

"Both dudes that gave it to me weren't exactly strangers."

"Ah, good point. Don't take candy from anyone!"

We giggled. Enjoying the ambiance, we finished our dinner. It was nice not to be alone. The backyard seemed like a new place with good company.

"So, is it true? Some kids made posts on Yipper about how your dad's a famous crime lord or something, and that you guys were only in Noxhelm for a federal protection program. He's way cool, by the way."

I peered over my shoulder to ensure he wasn't standing around. He wouldn't have liked for me to talk about him.

"Partially true. Yes, we were in Noxhelm because my dad was going to be a witness, but that went away. Yes, my father heads an organization once known for engaging in some illegal activity. But they only got bad once Vincent Byrne took over after my great-grandpa passed away. My dad's turned it around, and everything's legit. They do loans and dabble with some gambling things, I dunno any details, but they don't deal guns or drugs, that's for sure. I wouldn't call him a crime lord." I smiled. "So how are things back in Noxhelm?"

"Your old house was torn down."

"Ah, Ripper House is gone? Why?"

"City Council had a meeting with the HOA of our neighborhood. Funny thing, we'd lived there most of my life, and my parents lived next door to the place but never heard the rumors. They didn't even know about crazy Tabatha. Once they found out, they flipped."

"Oh my. It seemed like everyone at school knew about it."

She shrugged her shoulders with a smirk as she pulled her blanket up to her chest. "My parents didn't really hang around anyone locally. They both work forty-five minutes away, and just always stick together, don't leave the house much unless they're traveling abroad. They're totally unaware of their surroundings." She laughed. "I'm unsure of what went down, but the HOA purchased Tabatha Gill's home for triple its worth. Bulldozers arrived the next week and tore both houses down. They planted a bunch of trees and put in a playground. There's a plaque with Merry Biggs's picture on it with a blurb about the devastation that illegal drugs can have on families. They named it Merry Biggs Park."

"Wow, that's crazy." I pushed away my tray and set my lounger to recline. "Did Stephanie ever get charged with Merry's murder?"

"I believe the case was dropped. She's at a community college in San Francisco. Her mom's a cop, and her dad's one of the most powerful people in Noxhelm — he's the mayor. Probably coached by a parent, her little sister never backed up the story about the binder or the candy. All the DA had was a text uncovered from the investigation of Blaine's murder. It was a text to his best friend where he admitted to selling Stephanie two doses of Lapse the same day Merry went nuts. Even though this text backs up the case against Stephanie, it's all circumstantial."

"At least people know what happened. I think that's all Merry ever wanted."

"What do you mean by that? How would you know Merry wanted that?"

My words had slipped from my tongue without a filter. I'd never told Andrea I had spoken to Merry's ghost. "Oh, I'm just saying if I were her, that's what I'd want — for people to know the truth of what happened and why I went nuts and shot my mom and her friends." I got up and walked over to the pool to dip my feet in the water.

"Can you get that thing wet?" She pointed to my ankle bracelet.

"Ah, yeah, it's water resistant."

She followed my lead, and we sat on the ledge with our legs dangling, eyeing a perfect view of the sunset with a fine steamy mist rising from the surface of the water. "So what ever happened to

Don, anyway? Did he get in a good school?"

"Ah, well, Lynda Green was awarded the inheritance that she and Blaine were up for with their great-aunt's estate. Lynda's loaded now. She's living in her mansion in Stanford, and since Don, her stepcousin, also got into Stanford, he's her new roommate."

"Good for them! I'm glad to see that both of them are living well and have bright futures. They deserve that." I paused as Chef Bobbi collected our dinner trays and asked us if we needed anything further. We declined, and he switched on the built-in tiki torches that surrounded the pool and dashed back inside. "Do you know what happened to Tabatha Gill? You said they bought her home, so where did she go?"

"No clue. The day after the sale, the moving truck arrived, and she was gone. That woman had such a tragic life; I don't blame her for wanting to leave Noxhelm. I feel sorry for ever making fun of her, you know. I don't know if I ever told you, but she had lived in your old house before. Her husband died from carbon monoxide poisoning from a broken heater while the family slept. Tabatha and her daughter were also poisoned, but they made it out okay. Her daughter was so upset about her father, she committed suicide four days later by taking a bunch of pills. Merry's family bought the house from her, and she moved into the small house next door. Merry befriended Ms. Gill after she discovered she could speak to Violet, Tabatha's daughter."

"Wait, Merry was talking to Tabatha's daughter?"

"Um, yes. And Ms. Gill was always hanging around the house until Merry's mom threatened to get a restraining order on the poor woman."

"You never told me that. How sad. But how did Merry speak to her daughter?" I knew the answer to the question, but I had to hear how Andrea would explain it.

"Duh, girl. That house is super haunted. Don't tell me you never saw ghosts there."

I smiled. It was going to take a pot of coffee and a sunrise to tell this story.

ABOUT THE AUTHOR

Dr. Bon Blossman is a published fiction author, and founder of the world's top murder mystery company, MyMysteryParty.com. She's a recording artist and a developmental physiologist. She is also an adjunct professor with decades of teaching experience at the college level, as well as teaching forensic science to high school students.

Dr. Bon Blossman completed her Bachelor of Science in Pre Medicine (Biology and Chemistry), her Master of Science in Biology (Microbiology) and her PhD in Biology (Integrative Developmental Physiology). She continued with a two-year postdoctoral fellowship in a developmental cardiovascular research program.

 Dr. Bon has held memberships with Beta Beta Beta Biological Honor Society, Gamma Sigma Epsilon Chemical Honor Society, Phi Kappa Phi Honorary Society, National Scholars Society and has been listed on the Cambridge Society's Who's Who List. She also has held memberships with the Society for Integrative and Comparative Biology (SICB), the American Association for the Advancement of Science (AAAS) and the American Institute for Biological Science (AIBS).

Since 1998, she has published over five scientific journal articles in the fields of microbiology, mammalogy, and physiology, including a landmark paper in metabolic allometry, with her most recent research focused on the development of the embryonic cardiovascular system. She has served as an ad hoc reviewer for the Royal Integrative Society. Dr. Bon currently lives in the state capital of Texas with her husband, son, and Doberman named Ozzy. Her daughter, son-in-law, and granddaughter live only a few hours away in Dallas, Texas.

Twitter @BonBlossman
Facebook: BonnieBlossman